CONVICT
me

USA Today Bestselling Author

J.L. BECK *and*
C. HALLMAN

Copyright © 2019 Beck & Hallman LLC
Editing by: Word Nerd Editing
Cover Design by: T. E. Black Designs
All rights reserved.
No part of this book may be reproduced in any form or by any electronic or mechanical means, including information storage and retrieval systems, without written permission from the author, except for the use of brief quotations in a book review.

AUTHORS NOTE

Note from The Authors

Thank you so much for picking up Convict Me. Cassy and I look forward to hearing your thoughts, and reading your reviews. With that said we would like to make a statement in regards to this book, and the series overall. The heroes in this book and series are not your typical heroes. They're unapologetic, dark, and sometimes uncaring, they're possessive, over the top, and growly. They will make you angry, they will do things that you do not like nor approve of…but that's the great thing about fiction. This is a crime romance series and thought each book is considered a standalone reading in order will offer a better reading experience. This book and series contains dark themes, including dubious content, as well as scenes of peril and violence. If you need a trigger warning when reading then do not read this book or series. Each book ends with its own happily ever after if that helps any.

If none of these things bother you then please continue forward, and of course happy reading!

XOXO

J.L. Beck & C. Hallman

1

ero

I TAP the pencil on the notepad so furiously, it's about to give way and break in half. Where is this stupid tutor girl? I glance down at my phone to check the time. Fifteen past six. She was supposed to be here fifteen minutes ago. Every minute I sit here, it makes me more irritated, more impatient.

This small room with its bare walls reminds me too much of the prison cells I spent the last seven years in. The seconds tick by slow. The walls feel like they're closing in around me—inching toward me like they are about to swallow me whole.

Not only am I one of the oldest students here, but also one of the dumbest. Thanks to the lack of proper education the justice system provided me with, I could barely pass my classes.

If it hadn't been Mom's wish for me to go to college, I would get up, walk my happy ass right off campus, and never look back.

I'm not here to make friends or kiss ass. Half the things I've seen and done, these assholes wouldn't be able to handle.

Death. Murder. Pain. Grief. These people have no idea the shit-balls life could throw at you.

The door handle to the room jiggles, and I sneer at it. I should just get up and walk out of here. I'm sure the girl isn't going to be coming anyway.

"Hi! I'm so sorry. I got lost, then…"

The words I intended to speak pause in thin air. All my irritation and anger disappears, replaced with something else—something I've never felt before.

It's an emotion I can't quite pinpoint. Instead of focusing on it, I take in the tiny woman before me.

She has fragile features, soft, doll-like. Coal black lashes frame her big blue eyes, and those eyes…fuck, they're fixated on mine, beckoning me onward. Her coffee-colored hair is braided over one shoulder. It looks soft. I want to run my fingers through it.

What the fuck? I shove the thought away. My gaze drops to her full lips, half parted with whatever words she'd planned to say.

She isn't wearing a speck of makeup. Her clothes aren't eye-catching and don't show off her body, but damn…she is perfect.

"I—I'm sorry…" Her creamy white cheeks grow pink with embarrassment.

"You're late," I announce gruffly, as if she didn't already know this.

She sighs, visibly trying to calm herself.

I've been through enough shit to know when someone is on the verge of a panic attack. The look in her doe eyes tells me she's close.

"Please don't tell anyone. I need this job. I really, really do." Tears form in those orbs, and the anguish in her voice tells me she isn't lying.

Fuck! This isn't what I need right now. I'm not in a good place, and the moment I open my mouth, I know I'll ask her what the hell her story is and how I can help her...and that's just not what I need.

Shutting my brain down, I let my dick talk for me. "Calm down. You can make it up to me, baby. I promise I won't tell anybody. All you need to do is come over here and kiss me."

Her eyes go impossibly wide at my request. "K-Kiss y-you?" she stutters, staring at me like I just asked her to get on her knees and give me a blow job.

Shit. The image of her sucking me off invades my mind, making it hard to think about anything but her plum, angel-like lips around my cock. Shifting in my seat, I try to ignore how uncomfortably hard my dick is pushing against the zipper of my jeans, begging for me to let him come out to play. "So, what will it be? Kiss me or possibly lose your job?" I know I'm being an unreasonable asshole, but it's hard to be anything else when that's what I've been for so long.

She inches forward, like a newborn deer taking its first steps. Her legs seem so wobbly and unsure. For a moment, I think she might fall, and prepare myself to catch her.

Never breaking eye contact, she makes it all the way in front of my chair without falling over her own two feet. She clenches the strap of her backpack so tight, her knuckles turn white and her hand quivers.

Fear shines prominent in her eyes, but there's also curiosity and excitement. I hold my hand out to her, and she looks down at it in wonder. Her fingers ease up on the strap before she lets her backpack slide down her shoulder and drop to the floor.

Her small, shaking hand reaches for mine. The second her soft hand touches my much larger, rougher one, her trembling subsides. I gently pull her down into my lap, and her leg brushes against my hardened dick, almost making me come in my pants.

Her pink cheeks turn into a fiery crimson when she feels the effect she has on me. My cock presses firmly against her thigh, but I don't care. I have no plans of hiding how she makes my body feel.

Her free hand lands on my shoulder as if it belongs there, and I realize it does.

She belongs to me. She is mine.

The words are foreign to me. I've never claimed a woman before, and I'm not sure how to feel about it.

My nostrils tingle as I inhale her sweet scent of vanilla and cinnamon. The aroma is something I already know will be forever embedded into my mind, always reminding me of this tiny little creature in front of me.

"I..." she starts.

I hold my finger up to her lips, silencing her. "Shhh. Just kiss me," I order.

I don't think she's even blinked since I've asked her for a kiss. Part of me wonders if she's going to go through with it. She closes her eyes, and I take in every tiny detail of her perfect features. Her long, dark lashes fan across her unblemished skin, and she adorably puckers her lips just slightly as she inches toward me.

She's so fucking adorable, I feel like an even bigger asshole for making her do this. But my selfish needs outweigh my moral code—something that's partially broken anyway. I want to keep my eyes open, not wanting to miss a second of seeing her, but once her lips touch mine, I'm no longer able to do so.

Her lips graze mine, hesitant. She kisses with a softness that tells me one thing: she's innocent. My eyes flutter closed, and my brain ceases to work. The world could have stopped spinning, and I wouldn't have noticed.

My pulse pounds in my ears, and I fist the soft fabric of her shirt. She's tiny, so fucking tiny, and it breaks down all my walls. The urge to devour, protect, and secure her consumes me, but I reign it in. I'm not the kind of man for someone like her. I'm a broken bastard, hardened by prison and life. I'm also selfish, and feelings aren't something I can spare right now.

She softly moans into my mouth, and a zing of excitement slams into my dick. Her lips are soft, so fucking soft, so I press mine greedily against hers, eating up her moans and gasps. I release her shirt and work my way up her body until I'm cradling her face in my hands. It only takes a second for her to realize how wild this could get. She pulls away, a flustered expression marring her beautiful features.

Beep. Beep. Beep. The sound fills the small room. Without thought, she jumps off my lap and scurries back a few feet, clutching her backpack to her chest, looking at me like I stole her innocence.

It's irritating as fuck. She's the one who jumped in my lap and kissed me. "Don't look at me like I killed your fucking dog. I kissed you, and from the way you pawed at me, I doubt you didn't want it," I growl in frustration, a cross between need and anger spiraling out of control.

She flinches, her eyes going wide as she pulls her phone out of her backpack and disables the annoying beep. With unsteady hands, she gets out her books and lays them on the table next to my notepad. She opens them, turning to a page.

I know she is talking, probably about whatever she is supposed to tutor me in, but I can't take my eyes off her. Her angelic voice reaches my ears, but I can't make out the words.

I don't know how much time passes. Could be a minute or an hour. I'm suddenly pulled out of my trance when the door swings open and a scrawny, dark-haired kid appears in the doorway.

"Hey, are you Elyse? My tutor?" he asks, pushing his glasses up on his nose.

Nerd. What the fuck does he need a tutor for? The fact that the fucker said her name hits me. *Elyse?* I let her name roll off my tongue.

It didn't even occur to me to ask her for her name, not even when I was kissing the living daylights out of her.

"Yes, yes I am." She smiles, but it doesn't meet her eyes. It's fake, and a look I'm sure she's given many times. "We were just finishing up." She turns her attention back to me briefly, pointing to her book. "You got all of this?"

I almost laugh. She can't possibly think I heard a single word she said. I didn't get a fucking thing from that book.

Shaking my head, I watch her swallow hard and can't help but imagine her swallowing something else. *Fuck me.* I need to get out of here and get her out of my head before this whimsical siren becomes the death of me.

I shove away from the table and stand to grab my still-empty notepad before rushing out of the room and slamming the door shut behind me. I make it exactly three steps down the hall when the thought of her being alone in that room with another guy brings me to a halt.

It's unsettling how much this little waif of a woman affects me.

Gritting my teeth, I do what every sane man would and walk right back to the door I just came from, positioning myself in front of it. I sigh, leaning my shoulder against the door. I'm close enough to hear them talking inside, and that comforts me.

Time seems to stand still. I know what I'm doing is wrong. I don't know this girl. I don't know a damn thing about her, but I want to—and that's enough to keep me planted right where I am.

Waiting. Listening. Watching.

2

lyse

I BARELY MAKE it through the next tutoring session. My mind is still reeling, my lips tingle, and my heart is doing somersaults in my chest. I'm all out of sorts—because of him. *Hero.* That can't really be his name, right? Questions swirled inside my head. Who is he? Why did he ask me to kiss him?

What just occurred between us was strange...like a chemical reaction—one I want to happen again and again. I try hard to focus on Lenny and the questions he's asking me, but I can't, and it's frustrating. I need this job and the money it offers to keep going to school.

"Are you listening to anything I'm saying, Elyse?" Lenny sounds annoyed. When I look up from the textbook, his expression confirms it.

"Uh, yes—I'm sorry." My cheeks heat.

"Hey..." Lenny gives me a reassuring smile, "it's okay. We

can pick up where we left off later. I've got some stuff I need to do today, okay?"

I don't want to end our session, not when we still have thirty minutes left, but I'm on edge. I can't hear, can't breathe—everything feels all out of sorts. "Okay." I sigh. "I'm sorry, though. Truly. I don't know what is going on with me today," I lie. It has everything to do with that Hero guy. He's tall, dark, and handsome, with an edge of danger—everything my parents would hate.

Lenny packs up his stuff, and I follow suit. I can still taste the kiss of Hero's lips on mine. Can still feel the warmth of his muscled body. I've never been kissed before, but even with my non-existing experience, I know what we shared is more.

Lenny turns the door handle, pulling it open, and a body crashes into the room. I stumble back to avoid being smashed.

When I realize it's Hero, I lick my lips and gaze up at him.

He's so brooding. Dark, coal black hair as unruly as his attitude. His eyes are a soft green, that give away nothing. He's lean but built. I wonder just what it'd feel like if I took my fingers and ran them under his shirt.

Shaking his head, Lenny pushes past Hero and I with a grumbling, "Thank you."

I want to shout for Lenny, tell him not to leave me alone with Hero again, but the words never come out. My thoughts shift as I feel Hero's heated gaze on my skin.

What the hell is he still doing here? Was he waiting for me?

His gaze is so intense, it has me in a trance, and I can't help but look up at him.

"Are you afraid of me?" His voice is low, sinister even.

My mouth goes dry, as if someone just shoved an entire bag of cotton balls in it, making it impossible for me to speak. Not that I could if I wanted to. *What am I supposed to say?* I'd never in my entire life had an encounter with a man, and now, I'm having a complete out-of-body experience with one.

Finally getting up the courage to speak, I drop my gaze to the floor. "Should I be?" I don't want to look at him when he tells me yes, because even I can feel it—the danger, the anger. It rolls off him and slams into me like waves against the shoreline.

"I don't know yet... What I do know is I'm intrigued by you."

Intrigued? What does that mean? My roommate has talked numerous times about men wanting to sleep with her, but I'd never heard her say something about them being intrigued by her. I'm a nobody, so him being interested is surprising.

My head pounds. The entire situation is something I can't quite grasp onto. Hero is intense—far too intense for me. I need to walk away from him, need to put some distance between us.

"I want to see you again, and I know the perfect insurance to be sure I will."

My eyebrows furrow as he leans into my body, casting a dark shadow over me. His scent of cinnamon and wood tickles my nose. "Of course you'll see me again. I-I'm your t-tutor," I stutter, trying to keep the conversation casual. I've already spent way too much time in this man's company. If my father were here, he'd be picking up the bible to pray for him.

Hero smiles, and it's real, heartfelt even—it takes my breath away.

"I don't want to see you just between the four walls of that room, Elyse. I want to see you...like *really* see you."

His words vibrate through me, frightening me and exciting me all at once. I've never dated an honest to god man so I'm not sure what's expected of me. Do I agree? Disagree? Where I come from, women do as they're told, when they're told. Choices are not something given to us, so having a choice in this matter confuses me.

After a minute of eerie silence and intense staring, I force my legs to move forward. I step around him, fully expecting him to stop me, but he doesn't. I walk away faster than usual, knowing he's watching me leave. I can feel his eyes inside me, rattling me to the core.

I make it back to my dorm in record time. Taking two steps at a time, I turn and all but run to my door. I unlock it and walk inside before shutting it behind me, my lungs expanding for the first time in hours as I suck in precious oxygen.

"Hey you."

A loud shriek escapes my throat before I see Tasha, my roommate, sitting on her bed.

She raises an eyebrow.

"Sorry. I didn't see you there," I manage to get out, my hand clutching my chest. If I make it through this day without dying, I'll be shocked.

"Are you okay? You look like you might've seen Channing Tatum running around campus," she jokes.

Tasha knows about my family, so she understands me better than anyone here. But that doesn't mean I want to tell her about Hero.

"I'm fine. I was just in a rush to get back here," I say, knowing Tasha can see straight through my lie. She doesn't let me sugarcoat anything and lying in general is hard for me.

She rolls her eyes, but doesn't push. Thank goodness for that.

"Tonight, I'm taking little miss innocent to her first college party."

I blink slow, trying to comprehend what I just heard. "Did you just say party? Like the kind with drinking and boys?"

Tasha nods, a grin on her face.

"Yeah, I think I'll just stay here where it's safe."

Tasha stands with both hands on her hips, giving a look that says *oh no you don't.*

Compared to Tasha, I don't stand a chance. She's beauty and brains—a blonde bombshell with killer legs and even better body, so when she smiles, it seems like the sun is coming out. She shines light on even the worst moments, and from what I've seen, makes the best of everything.

"Safe?" She giggles. "Our dorm room isn't safe, girlfriend. If you won't come with me, I'll just bring the party to you."

I move away from the door and carry my bag over to the couch. Our dorm is small, with a tiny little kitchen and even smaller bathroom. It's a tight living space, but it's home, and it's mine...well, and Tasha's.

"No..." I shake my head. "I'll just go with you. If I don't and something happens to you, I'll feel guilty."

Tasha moves from where she's standing and comes over by me.

In her eyes, I see concern, and truthfully, I don't want to address it.

"You need this, Elyse. You really do. Maybe you don't think so, but it's important. All your life, you've lived under the rules of your father. Now, there are no rules. Now, you can do what and *who* you want." She winks.

I purse my lips. "I am not going to sleep with anyone. Not now, tomorrow, or ever. No one is interested in me." *Except Hero.* But I don't say that part out loud. The less Tasha knows about him, the better.

"No one is interested because they don't even know you exist. Put on a sexy outfit, let me do your makeup and hair, and we can bring the sex to you."

I cringe at the word. "No, Tasha. I don't want sex." Even saying it feels weird. Sex in my family is something you don't do 'til you're married—and you definitely don't sleep with anyone but your husband after that.

My father would probably have a stroke if he found out what took place behind the scenes at college.

"Everyone wants sex, and I mean *everyone*," she whispers, dragging me toward her closet.

There are various dresses and shirts hanging up, but none

of them look appealing to me. I'm not the partying type. I'm lucky to even be able to wear jeans instead of the floor-length dresses my father required since the day I started walking.

Tasha sifts through the clothing before pulling out a pair of black flats, black skinny jeans, and a white flowy blouse that will show off my boobs.

"I can't wear that," I hiss.

Tasha raises a brow, giving me a look that says *put it on or else*. After standing there for a few minutes with my arms crossed over my chest, I give in.

I eye myself in the mirror. Up. Down. And back again. It's so strange what a change in clothing can do for someone.

Tasha sees me checking myself out and smiles. "Girl, if you don't walk out of that party with at least three cocks trying to poke you, then those bastards are blind and their penises are broken."

I giggle. Her words are crude, but also make me feel like the young college student I'm supposed to be. Tasha does my makeup and hair, curling the ends slightly. By the time she's done, I feel like a completely different person.

I stare at my reflection. My parents would never approve of the woman I am right now. They'd never approve of the clothes, the makeup, or the hair, and this fact alone leaves me feeling guilty.

It's hard to leave old habits when they've been your structure of life forever. But that guilt dissipates when my thoughts turn to Hero. What would he think if he saw me?

"If you're done drooling over your own reflection, can we go?"

I roll my eyes as a bubble of laughter escapes my red painted lips. "Yes, Tasha, we can go. God forbid the dicks get there before you do."

Tasha gasps as her hand clutches her chest. "Did you just say dicks? Sweet baby Jesus, I've officially corrupted you!"

Her words earn her another eye-roll as we head out of the dorm toward the frat houses on University Street.

Music blasts through the speakers as we walk into the "football" house. According to Tasha, it's where all the football players live, and from the looks of it, I believe her. The place smells of beer and sweat, but that could just be all the bodies and beer sloshing around. Tasha pulls me through the crowd toward the kitchen. There are bottles of liquor everywhere, beer cans, and red solo cups.

Breathe, Elyse. It's just a party.

Forcing air into my lungs, I watch as Tasha tells some guy manning the drinks what we want.

He scoffs at her, but winks at me when my eyes lift to his.

He's cute enough, but he's not Hero. I shake the thought away. I don't even know him. He could be a mass murderer.

The guy in front of me hands me a cup filled with red liquid. My nose wrinkles as I smell the drink before taking a sip of it. As soon as I taste it, I want more. The flavor explodes against my tongue. I've never tasted something so delicious before. But I don't even get a moment to enjoy the rest of my drink because a hand comes out of nowhere, slapping my cup from my grasp.

The colorful, fruity liquid spills all over my clothes and the floor.

"Are you fucking stupid?"

I don't even need to turn around to see where that hand or voice came from. The hair stands up on the back of my neck and goosebumps spread out all over my skin.

It's him.

I stare down at my empty hand, still forming a half circle as if the glass hadn't vanished.

What just happened?

"I asked you a question. Are you stupid? Don't you know

you never drink anything a guy hands you at a party?" he snarls.

I lift my gaze to his. His eyes are dark and look almost black as his eyebrows pull together in anger. He looks past me, scanning the room for something.

Confusion settles into my brain. A second later, he finds whatever or whoever, because his eyes go from dark to midnight black as he steps past me, zeroing in on the guy who made my drink.

Like a wild animal on the hunt, he walks over to him.

The guy turns, and his eyes fill with pure fear as Hero wraps his hand wrapped around his throat.

"Please, man," he begs, his voice nothing more than a wheeze.

Hero swings back his free arm and his fist connects with the guy's cheekbone at full force. I'm halfway across the room, but I swear I can hear the bone crunch.

The guy's eyes roll back, and his whole body goes limp. With a loud thud, he hits the floor.

The room goes quiet, and all eyes are on Hero. My mouth is still hanging wide open as Hero makes his way back toward me.

Fear is a real emotion, and one I'm feeling it to the core. I take a small step back for every one of his large strides, like I would have a chance to get away. It's such a silly thought, but one I'd consider if my eyes would remain focused for less than half a second.

A moment later, his hands are around my arms. He's ushering me through a door and outside.

My feet can barely keep up with his rushed pace. If it weren't for his strong hold on me, I would have fallen on my face by now. "What was wrong with the drink and where are you taking me?" I ask, when I realize he's walking in the opposite direction of my dorm.

Oh no. I'm being kidnapped. Everything my father ever said to me about the world is true.

"My place," he says, matter of fact.

I know I should be terrified right now. I should be running and blowing that stupid rape whistle they gave me at orientation, but something tells me I'm going to be fine. My vision is blurry, and my stomach rolls with each step we take.

We walk a few more minutes before I start feeling really weird. My legs wobble, and my head feels like it's filling up with air. "I feel weird," I admit, and even my voice sounds off. "What's happening to me?" I whine.

Hero studies me for a long moment, his arm tightening around my waist. "Shhh, it's okay. Nothing is going to happen to you. Not while you're with me," he says, his voice low and tone calming.

My brain says I shouldn't trust him, but my gut says he's telling me the truth.

I'm fine. He's got me.

3

ero

By the time we get to my apartment complex, Elyse is so out of it, I have to carry her up the stairs. I hold her against my chest, cradling her. Her small frame fits perfectly into my arms. Her soft curves mold against my body. We fit perfectly together, like she's the puzzle piece I wasn't even aware I was missing.

I manage to unlock the door and switch on the light without having to set her down. Using my foot, I kick the door shut behind me, then click the lock into place. As soon as the world is shut out, a sense of calm washes over me.

I've got her, here, in my apartment.

A small moan escapes her mouth, and the sensual sounds travel straight to my dick.

Not now, asshole.

Pushing the need down, I carry her into my bedroom and place her on my bed. Her eyes are only halfway open, but her soft gaze follows me around the room.

I walk around the bed, trying to decide what to do next. Her pants are wet and sticky from the spilled drink—the drink I spilled. I scold myself. I should take them off. Just to get her more comfortable.

Then again...

My jaw clenches as I make a choice. Leaning over her, I unbutton her skinny jeans. She doesn't say anything, but her chest rises and falls in quick succession.

"I'm not going to hurt you, and I'm not going to touch you unless you want me to. I'm just getting these off you." I swallow as I pull down the zipper, careful not to touch anything more than I need to, even though every fiber in my body wants nothing more than to touch her anywhere I can.

I dip my fingers into her waistband and pull her pants down.

Light blue cotton panties come into view as I skim those jeans off her legs inch by inch. Her legs are slender and pale, just like the rest of her body. By the time I manage to get her pants off, my dick is so hard, it hurts.

Down, boy.

I can't have her. Not now. Not like this. She's only half awake, and I have no idea if she'll remember any of this tomorrow. I can't take advantage of her, and I won't.

Her eyes are still fixed on mine, and I am more than glad to see there is no fear left in them. It's probably just the drug circling through her system, but I don't care. I'll take it. Her trusting gaze means the world to me at this moment.

It's been so long since anyone has looked at me like this, I almost forgot what it felt like. To be trusted...to be wanted.

I sit down next to her on the bed, gazing down at the flowery blouse hugging her frame. The tops of her breasts are exposed, and I wonder how nice they would feel in my hands. I'm sure they would fit perfectly—just like everything else.

Fuck, she is perfect for me.

My hands move on their own accord, hovering over the buttons on her blouse.

She would probably be more comfortable if I took that off as well. I start unbuttoning her shirt from the top and work my way down until every single one is undone.

Her shirt falls open, revealing a matching light blue bra. My fingers glide over her feather-like skin as I slide the thin fabric down her arms.

I stop to gaze down at the goddess lying in front of me. I need to stop. I need to get away before I go too far. Turning my head, I push myself off the bed.

"Please," she whispers so softly, I almost didn't hear her.

I twist back to face her, finding her eyes pleading and fragile little hand reaching for me.

I'm not sure what she's pleading for. Hell, she might not even know herself. All I know is my heart just stopped beating and jump started itself into an unnatural rhythm.

I take her hand and let her pull me down next to her. She turns her head toward me, but it's not enough. I grasp onto her bare hip and pull her onto her side so we are facing each other. I know I need to stop touching her, but the desire is just so overwhelming. I reach for her face, cupping her smooth cheek in my hand.

"Have you ever done anything like this? Been touched or claimed by a man?" I swallow, knowing a part of me will break in two if she says yes. I want to be the man to fuck her for the first time, to devour her pussy and claim her as a man should.

"No. Never," she finally answers, her voice small and timid, unsure.

Happiness pools in my belly. "Do you want me to touch you now?" I croak, the question hanging in the air between us. I'm not a good man. I'm not kind or gentle either, but I want to be. For her. I want to be everything I've never been before.

"Yes," she whimpers, her eyes pleading, as if she wants me as badly as I want her.

That simple word is all I need for that thread of restraint to rip. I reach behind her, undoing the clasp of her bra before I move her onto her back.

Hovering over her, I pull the bra off, revealing the most perfect pair of tits I have ever laid eyes on. Two delicious round mounds with a small pink taut nipple on each, begging to be in my mouth.

I don't leave them waiting long. Bringing my mouth to her breast, I wrap my lips around one of the stiff tips. She moans, sending all the blood left in my brain straight to my cock.

Using my hand, I seek out her other breast and roll her nipple between two fingers while I suck the other one in earnest.

Elyse arches her back, crushing my mouth to her tit. I know she wants this, I just don't know how much of this is the drugs and how much is her. I can only let this go so far. She's innocent, naive, and I don't want her to regret this.

A voice in the back of my mind is still telling me to stop, but every one of her needy moans pushes that voice farther and farther away, until it vanishes altogether.

"Kiss me." Her voice is breathless.

I release her tit from my mouth with a loud pop. Gazing down into her eyes, I know I want this. I want it so fucking bad, it hurts. But I've gotta stop.

This is her first time experiencing something, and I want her to remember it—remember me. Pressing my lips against hers, I kiss her with every fiber of my being. When she lifts her arms, wrapping them around my neck, molding us together, I pull away. I have to.

My cock's stiffer than hell. It's getting harder and harder to remain in control.

Elyse whines in disappointment, a frown pulling at her plump lips.

I think about lying next to her and just going to sleep, but there's no way I'll be able to get a minute of rest with this raging hard-on. "I'm going to go take a shower. I'll be back in a little bit," I whisper into her hair before moving down to place another kiss to her lips.

Her eyes flutter closed, and she murmurs something beneath her breath.

I grab my comforter to cover her up before I disappear into the bathroom. I've never smiled so much in my life. Hell, I've never been happier. It's a strange feeling…happiness, that is.

When you grow up the way I did, you question everything—good, bad—and are ready at any given moment for disappointment because you're used to it. I strip out of my jeans, t-shirt, and boxers to eye myself in the mirror.

I've got a couple tattoos, but my best feature is the piercing at the tip of my cock. I think of Elyse's expression when she sees it for the first time. Will she feel fear or arousal? I don't want to scare her away, but the things I want from her aren't something I'm sure she can deliver.

I turn on the shower and step into the spray. It's cold for a second, then turns hot. Resting with my back against the tiles, I take my length into my hand, close my eyes, and shove the thoughts away. Elyse is what I want…what I need. She makes up for all the bad I've done in my life.

But will she want me when she finds out I'm a killer?

I hiss out in pleasure as I stroke myself, up and down, up and down, my muscles tightening. My hold tightens as my hand slips over the head and back down.

My thoughts shift to Elyse. Her perfect lips. The way her eyes sparkle when she looks at me. Even with fear in her eyes, she's the most beautiful woman I've ever laid eyes on.

My jaw clenches, and my strokes become more furious as

images of Elyse beneath me fill my mind, her pussy stretching and taking my cock as I pump into her.

Her moans of pleasure, her pleading for more, the erotic look in her eyes as she falls apart all over my cock. I wonder what her nails will feel like raking over my skin.

I feel the build deep in my balls as I curl my toes into the tub, feeling my insides spiral out of control. Air fills my lungs, but never fully inflates them.

I feel out of control. I pump harder, and harder, I groan, the pleasure encompassing me all at once. Sticky ropes of cum hit the wall while my body shakes with aftershocks, my muscles tense.

I sigh, sagging completely against the wall. This woman... she's ruining me, fucking ruining me, and the worst part is I want her to keep doing it.

I want to be better. I want to make her happy. But most of all, *I want her.*

4

lyse

I know something is off before I even open my eyes. The bed feels different, warmer. The comforter feels rougher, and it doesn't smell like my lavender laundry detergent.

My eyes open slowly, feeling dry and icky. I don't start panicking until I'm able to take in the unfamiliar room. My heart starts racing, pumping blood into every muscle in my body. Sitting up in a flash, the comforter slides down to my belly. I'm wearing a shirt I'm one hundred percent certain isn't mine. A hundred little snapshots from last night enter my mind at the same time.

Not one of them makes sense.

Someone stirring next to me grabs my undivided attention. I look beside me and find a large body half covered up with the same blanket I'm using. His bare, broad shoulders and tousled dark hair is all I see.

Clasping the blanket around my body, I jump up, trying to get away. My still clumsy feet get wrapped up in the comforter, making me tumble off the bed. With a loud thud, I land on the floor.

"Shit, are you okay?" Hero's voice sounds concerned as he stirs from sleep. The next moment, he's by my side, kneeling next to me.

Tears start to run down my cheek uncontrollably.

What have I done?

I've given up my virginity to someone I barely know, and I don't even remember it.

"Hey. Don't cry." Hero holds my face in his large hands, wiping my tears away with his thumbs.

His touch sends shivers of pleasure down my spine. The feeling feels familiar and some of the images from last night come to me more clearly.

Images of him taking my clothes off, touching me, kissing me, and, oh god, me begging him... *What was I begging him to do?* I cringe. It wouldn't surprise me if he didn't want to see me again after last night.

I open my mouth to say something, but before I can, he picks my still wrapped up body up like I weigh nothing and deposits me back on the bed.

His bed.

Scurrying backwards, I try to calm myself by lifting my gaze to his. There's a softness in his eyes I want to reach out and touch. Still, the question on the tip of my tongue remains. I ask it before I lose the courage.

"Did you...? I mean, did we...?" I trail off, dropping my eyes to the floor. Guilt and shame coat me from the inside out. I don't remember going that far, but my mind is still a jumbled mess. My body still feels the same, and there's no soreness between my legs...but that doesn't mean anything, right? Bile rises in my throat—and I panic. Had I just accused Hero of raping me? My head is a mess, my thoughts swirling all together.

"Have sex?" he finishes my question, his tone a bit condescending. "No. When I'm inside your virgin pussy for the first time, I want to be certain you feel, and remember, every single thing."

My cheeks heat.

Will there be a first time?

I remember my reaction to him last night, the pleasure that coursed through my veins, the way my body lit up like a Christmas tree at the press of his lips and touch of his hands.

"You're thinking about it now, aren't you? Thinking about how you almost gave yourself to a monster—a man you don't even fucking know, a man who could've raped you, violated you, took your innocence and hurt you." His words are dark, his gaze even darker, almost manic.

A shiver of fear goes down my spine.

He's so hot and cold. On and off. He gives me whiplash, yet I feel drawn to him, like a moth to a flame. I've never met a man like him before, but I want to know more about him, what makes him this way.

"I wasn't," I lie, knowing I'm not good at it.

A humorless laugh escapes his lips. "You're a shit liar, Elyse."

I can tell he's hurt by my response, and I'm not sure how to deal with it. "I didn't—I mean…I don't think you'd do that, but I don't know you, and I don't…" I stumble over my words, unsure of how to make this all right. It started with a forced kiss, and now, I'm here in his bed with him.

"If I wanted to fuck someone who was unconscious, I could've picked any of the chicks at that party last night. I brought you here because I wanted to protect you—I had to protect you. I didn't intend on touching you, Elyse...and I wouldn't have even if you had begged me to," he grits out.

He's battling with his own emotions.

His fists are clenched at his sides, his face contorted in anger, his lips almost in a snarl.

Anger terrifies me. It gives me anxiety, but a small part of me knows Hero would never hurt me.

Hesitantly, I lift my hand and rest it against his thigh to reassure him I'm not afraid of him. The air sizzles between us as his eyes move from my hand up to my face. When he lifts his hand, I flinch.

The anger in his eyes intensifies when he sees my reaction. "I'm not a good man—not at all. I've done things. Seen things. I've killed people."

The air in my lungs stills, blood pounds in my ears. The need to run is so strong, but I remain kneeling beside him, my body trembling.

"But I will never, ever fucking hurt you, Elyse. Never."

The conviction in his voice makes me believe him.

God, there has to be something wrong with me for believing him, a man I don't even know, but I do. "I know."

The smile Hero gives me is grim. "If you knew, you wouldn't be trembling or have that look in your eyes that says you're ready to bolt out the door."

"This is just all new to me," I sigh. "This is my first experience out in the real world. The last eighteen years of my life I've been under my parents' thumb, living the life they wanted me to live, cooking, cleaning, never asking questions, and only speaking when spoken to."

Hero's gaze goes wide, and he runs a hand through his hair as if it's a nervous tick.

His dark locks look so soft, I want to reach out and run my own fingers through them.

"What do you mean this is your first experience in the real world? Were you in like a fucking cult or something?"

I think about his response for a second. A cult? I had never heard the word before.

"I don't know what a cult is, but I can tell you things weren't fun, and they were never easy." I cringe, thinking of all the times I got the belt for something one of my siblings had done. Blame was placed on everyone. Yes, we all got food and a bath, but we were never really loved, not like most parents loved their kids, and we were never given a choice. Never.

"That explains a lot..." Hero sighs.

I wrinkle my nose at his response. "What do you mean that explains a lot? Do I have a sign on my forehead or something?" I smile, feeling the tension seep out of the air.

Hero smirks, pushing from the bed.

I stare at his ass as he walks away, my insides turning to mush as I watch his muscles move, my mind thinking of all the different ways I could use my mouth on him. My thoughts shift when he walks out of the room.

As soon as he's out of sight, I scurry from the bed, find my pants on the floor, and pull them on. I gaze down at the shirt I'm wearing. I suppose I'll keep it and give it back to him later since I have nothing else to wear.

"What did you mean?" I ask once more as I run into the kitchen.

Hero shrugs, pulling out a carton of orange juice as he leans against the counter. "It doesn't really mean anything. You just have this innocence about you. You're sweet and quiet, and it fits your personality."

I feel slightly insulted at his words. "Well, excuse me for fitting my personality. I couldn't exactly tell you were a murderer from your personality."

Hero raises a thick brow. "It's not like I wanted to be one. I wasn't born a killer, Elyse."

I nibble on my bottom lip, feeling guilty for saying something so harsh. "What happened?" I ask, afraid to know, but curious enough to ask.

"I'm not sure you're ready to hear this," he states, like he actually has a choice whether he tells me or not.

"All my life, I've been told no. All my life, people have hidden things from me. Don't do that to me, Hero. Don't hide something that made you who you are today."

"I don't want you to be afraid of me or your perspective of me to change. I've done some bad shit. I know those things don't define me as a person, but meeting you has changed me. Changed my thinking, my wants, needs." He gives me a dejected look.

I almost feel sorry for even asking, but I want this, this friendship, this relationship, whatever it may be.

I cross the space separating us and place my hand against his bare chest. His skin is warm beneath my palm and smells clean. My eyes take forever to make it up to his face. When I do, I see he's been watching me the whole time.

Way to go, Elyse.

"I want to know you...like really know you. I've never had a friend, except Tasha, and I've definitely never had a guy friend." I smile up at him, praying he tells me a morsel about who he is.

Hero lifts his hand, gripping me by the chin very gently, forcing me to look into his eyes. "I'm not a good man, Elyse. But that doesn't mean I'll run you away. It doesn't mean I'm not selfish enough to take you or want you, because I am. But I won't tell you I'm good. I don't want you afraid of me, but there are things I've done you will fear. There are things I may do to protect you that will scare you."

I nod my head as well as I can within his grasp. "I'm sure whatever you did, you had good reason to do it." I don't really understand why it matters, what his past has to do with our future.

He glances away briefly, and when his eyes come back to mine, there's a different look in them, a faraway look, like he's somewhere else altogether. "I killed a man. A man who abused me and my mother. I killed him, and honestly, I'd do it again if given the chance."

I blink slowly, digesting every word. He killed a man. A man who abused him. A man who abused his mother. I almost sigh in relief. He's not a killer because he wants to be... "You were protecting yourself. Protecting your mother," I announce, like he doesn't already know that.

He releases his hold on my chin, but continues to look at me, making sure I see and hear every word he says. "I went to prison for it. It changed me. It broke me. It made me cold, cruel, and angry. I'm always angry. Always," he sighs. "Except with you."

My heart flips inside my chest. I want to kiss him again.

The sound of a phone ringing pulls me from the trance I'm in and I realize it's my cellphone going off. I blink and run in the direction of the sound. This is bad, so bad. It could be my parents, or Tasha. "Oh my gosh. I forgot about Tasha," I mumble, spotting my phone on Hero's dresser as well as my wallet. Tasha's name scrolls across the screen, and I damn near sigh in relief. At least it's not my parents.

I fire off a quick text telling her I'll be home soon.

"I need to go back to my place," I yell over my shoulder.

"Perfect. I'll take you there now."

I hear his response and frown. My heart's still beating like crazy inside my chest and I don't want this moment with him to end. I have questions, so many. Questions for him, for myself. *What would my parents think about him?*

I nibble on my bottom lip. Nothing good, I know for sure. They would never, ever approve of someone like Hero. But this knowledge draws me even more to him. He's everything my parents warned me of, everything they resent in a man, and maybe, that's exactly why I need him. *Why I'm drawn to him.*

"Ready?" Hero's voice vibrates through me, and I look up to see him standing in the doorway. The look on his face tells me he doesn't want this morning to end either, and that's enough proof for me to come back again.

5

ero

I walk across the campus square in a shit mood. It's been nearly a week since I've heard from Elyse, and it's pissing me off. I consider skipping my study session with her, but remember the way she reacted at being late and how she needed the job so badly, she kissed a complete stranger.

The thought makes me smile, how easily she was persuaded into kissing me. It's merely another example of why she needs my protection. Such a precious flower in a venomous world.

I remind myself how I had to cement my feet to the floor so I wouldn't go to her. I want to see her up close, not just from the dark corners I've been hiding in when I follow her to and from classes.

I want to talk to her, not just hear her voice from afar, and I definitely want to kiss her again, but I need to give her a chance to come to me first.

This needs to be her choice. I can't and won't push her into this. From the way the week has gone, it's starting to look like she isn't as interested in me as I thought she was. Which sucks. Really fucking bad.

I feel the dirty looks people are giving me as I walk across campus. It makes my skin crawl. Grown ass men switch to the other side of the street when they see me coming. Most people are just scared, and I can deal with that. What's harder is when I see the disgust written clearly on their faces.

I can't help but wonder what kind of looks people would give me if Elyse were walking beside me.

Would they judge her too?

I catch a glimpse of a familiar pair of eyes. I've only seen them briefly, and it takes me a moment to place them. It's Elyse's friend, I realize. The one from the party.

She obviously knows who I am, judging by the death stare I'm receiving right now. She glares at me like a lioness about to pounce, and for a minute, I really do think she will attack. She looks nothing like Elyse. There's no kindness in her features. In fact, she looks as if she's better than everyone else.

She flips her blonde hair over her shoulder as she pretends to be listening to something the guy next to her is saying, but I'm not stupid. Her eyes stay trained on me until I make it all the way up the library steps, the heat of her gaze telling me she doesn't approve of my kind.

I ignore everyone and everything as I shove my hands into the pockets of my jeans and walk in the direction of the study session rooms.

Fuck. I don't want to be here right now. I shouldn't be here right now.

When I get into the room, Elyse is already sitting at the table, her book open, her notes set out before her.

She looks up at me, her eyes full of dread. She shifts nervously in her chair when I take the seat next to hers. The tension is so thick, you can cut it with a knife. Questions rest against the tip of my tongue.

Why didn't she text me? Call me? Come over again? I clench my jaw to keep my mouth shut. She doesn't deserve my shitty attitude, even if she is the cause of it. Maybe she made her choice already. Maybe she decided she didn't want to hear from me anymore or want anything to do with me.

"I got some information about the areas you're struggling in," Elyse nearly whispers, her eyes back on the book in front of her.

My face deadpans, like there isn't anything else better we could be doing or saying. "Is that so?" I say through gritted teeth.

She seems taken aback by the anger in my voice.

What the hell was she expecting?

"Why are you mad at me? You're the one who made a bunch of empty promises, then just forgot about me." Her kissable lips are pulled taunt, and the crease in her forehead tells me she is frustrated.

"Forgot about you?" I sneer, unclenching my fists, only to clench them again.

How can she think I forgot about her when my every thought is about her? I wake up, I see her face. I close my eyes, I see her face. I'm fucking obsessed with her, with the need to protect her, be with her, inside her, beside her—it doesn't really fucking matter so long as she's there.

I'm scared shitless, and nothing scares me...except the small, five-foot-two girl in front of me and the power she has over me.

"I waited for you to come to me. To call me? I don't have your number," she whispers. "I don't know how any of this works, okay? I told you this is all new for me."

Her bottom lip trembles, and I feel like an even bigger asshole than I know I am.

She told me about her past. Maybe I shouldn't have assumed she knew I was giving her a choice in all this.

"You just left me."

Her words break my black heart in two. "I didn't leave you. I was with you all week." I grin at her. "You just didn't see me."

For the first time since I got here, a small smile tugs on her lips.

I can't take my eyes off her face. "I need you to tell me this is what you want. That I am what you want. I thought I could wait. I thought I could let you choose, but it's obvious that isn't going to happen given the circumstances right now." I shift in my seat and gaze deeply into her eyes, making sure she gets every single word I'm telling her. "I need you to understand that once you tell me, there is no going back. If you want this. Us. I will never let you go again. You'll be mine forever."

She pauses for just a moment, her eyes never wavering from mine.

I wait intently for her answer, knowing even if she says no, I can't let her go, not really.

"I want you. I want us."

I can tell the exact moment my heart stops beating for myself and starts beating for her. *Only her.* There's a shift in the air, a tingle of excitement and a trickle of fear. As soon as her words reach my brain and my body starts working again, I lean into her face and press her lips to mine.

She moans into my mouth, and I have half the mind to pick her up and fuck her right here on the table. When her arms snake around my neck, pulling me closer, I almost do just that. I pull away just an inch to prevent me from doing anything I know I'll most likely regret later. "Let's go home," I say, getting up from my chair and tugging her with me.

"I-I can't go. I-I need this job, remember? I have other students and things to pay for and..." The proverbial reasons spill from her mouth so fast, my head spins.

"Don't worry about money. You don't need this job. All you need to know is I'll take care of you. No matter what, I'll be there for you."

I see the worry creep into her features. She doesn't believe me, and I understand why, but that doesn't make it any harder of a pill for me to swallow.

"I can't let you do that, Hero. I need to give Tasha half the rent every month. I need to pay for books and food. I appreciate you want to take care of me, but I left my home so I could prove I can take care of myself."

"I know you can take care of yourself. You don't have to prove that. Not to me or anyone else." I just want her with me so fucking much. I want to spend every minute of the day with her. "Move in with me," I blurt out.

"I don't know." She's visibly flustered.

I decide I better not push her any farther right now. Reeling in my need for her, I slump back into the chair, trying not to show my utter disappointment. I know I'm being a little unreasonable, but I need her to understand she belongs to me and I will do anything for her.

"How about this? You keep living with your friend in the dorm, but you will quit this job and start working as my personal tutor. Which, of course, will earn you a pay raise. I'll pay you top dollar," I snicker. "And know, if you ever change your mind on wanting to move in with me, say the word and I'll help you pack myself."

A wide smile spreads across her face, and I know she's going to say yes before she even opens her mouth. "Okay."

6

lyse

After our tutoring session, Hero insists on walking me back to the dorm. I would be lying if I said I didn't like the idea of him taking care of me since it would take a lot of the stress off me so I'll be able to concentrate more on my own studies.

Ironically, my parents believe men should take care of the women in their life anyway, but I highly doubt they had Hero picked out as a future husband. In fact, I know he's the exact opposite of what they would find acceptable.

I let the thoughts go, and together, we walk up the stairs leading to my dorm room. A part of me wonders if I should invite him into my room. All we've ever done is kiss and some light petting, maybe he's expecting more from me?

I told him I want this, whatever it is, to be his, does that mean—

Three steps before we reach the top of the stairs, my knees lock up, propelling me forward. My heart races inside my chest, and I feel like I'm on the verge of a panic attack. My arms fly up instinctively to brace myself from falling, but Hero's quick reflexes protect me. With one strong arm wrapped around me, he pulls me straight up on my feet and into his side.

"Are you okay?" Hero asks, searching my face for a response.

"I..." One single vowel is all I can get past the golf ball sized lump in my throat. My eyes never waver from the two figures standing in front on my dorm room door, their judgmental eyes staring me down like they're about to drag me away by my hair and lock me up in the church basement.

I can't breathe. My hands feel clammy, and my body is reacting in a way it never has before. There's fear, but there's something else beneath that.

What are my parents doing here?

Hero follows my gaze, and out the corner of my eyes, I see his eyebrows draw together. "Who is that?" he questions, not bothering to keep his voice down.

"*We* are Elyse's parents," my dad answers, like he's some kind of holy crusader.

My palms are sweaty, and my stomach twists into a nervous knot.

"And *you* are...?" my mom asks Hero, turning her nose up at him in disgust.

Hero doesn't seem the least bit intimidated or offended as he walks up to my dad. Holding his head high, shoulders squared, he stops in front of him, extending out his hand. "I'm Jonathan Miller, sir. It's nice to meet you."

I almost choke on the air in my lungs.

Hero's hand hovers in midair, my dad making no move to shake it. His facial expression and gesture say everything he'll never say. My dad thinks he is better than Hero, and by not shaking his hand, he's ensuring Hero knows it.

The shock I experienced a few moments ago transforms

and anger takes center stage. *How dare they treat him like he is less.* So what if he's not someone who would be considered suitable in our world. That doesn't mean he's a bad person or unworthy of respect.

"Mom, Dad, I wasn't expecting you to come for a visit," I snap, somehow finding my voice, the words twisted with anger.

I hate that Hero is meeting them. I never wanted him to meet them.

"Oh, dear, we just wanted to see how things were going. We were hoping you had come to your senses by now and would like to come back home with us." My mother's cheerful gaze and words snap me in two.

Anger pours from me.

Hero, who has long since dropped his hand, also changes moods. While we talk, my dad continues glaring at me and Hero with something that looks a whole lot like disgust and disappointment mixed together.

"Things are going great here. Matter of fact, I did come to my senses. I came to my senses the day I decided to go to college, so no, I am not planning on returning home, Mother." I don't know who is more surprised by my little outburst: me or my parents. But it sure does earn me a dirty look from them both. I can count on one hand the times I dared to raise my voice toward my parents—all of which ended with me getting a beating and going to bed hungry.

But he can't do that here, not now. Noticing my dad's hand twitch, I wait for him to pull out his belt and try to whip me with it. Instead, he just stands there, unmoving. This is the first time in my life I've seen my dad hesitant like this.

Looking into his eyes, I see something I've never seen in there before.

Fear.

Is he scared of Hero?

Considering the bulging vein on my father's forehead, I

would say he is angry enough to give me the whooping of a lifetime, but he makes no move to do so, which is strange. Without looking or thinking things through, I reach for Hero's hand. "Can I stay at your place?" I ask, briefly glancing up at him.

I know it's only stirring the pot and will make them angry, but the last thing I want to do is stay here in this dorm by myself after this encounter. If anything, I want to be closer to Hero, in his arms, wrapped up in his bed sheets.

My parents' eyes widen to the point where I worry about their eyeballs popping out.

"Of course, baby," Hero says sweetly, bringing our hands together.

"No, you may not go to his house with him!" my mother snarls, ready to slap me across the face. That's how it always works—a little discipline and we never ask a question or make a choice again. They beat us to bend at their will, but I'm not under their thumb anymore. I'm not a part of their sick, twisted games anymore.

"That is not your choice." Hero scowls.

My father takes a step forward, as if he's going to get in Hero's face. "You're not worthy of my daughter. Furthermore, how would your future husband feel about you being with another man?" My father directs his attention back to me.

I hate the way his eyes penetrate mine. He's trying to intimidate me, and it's working.

"She's promised to no one," Hero butts in once again. The air around him is cool, but his gaze it heated with anger. He wants to slug my father, I'm sure.

"She's promised to whomever I decide." My father takes a thunderous step forward and a part of me wonders if Hero will back down. I don't want Hero to fight with my parents, but it's inevitable, especially after the way they've looked down and acted toward him.

"I'll be the judge of that." Hero chuckles, a possessiveness in his eyes. Hero is possessive, intruding even, but his intentions are pure, and I know deep down he really is the hero he claims himself not to be.

"We—we really should go." I tug on Hero's hand, not wanting to continue the conversation with my parents any longer.

"Excuse me, young lady, but we drove an entire hour to see you. The least you could do is go to dinner with us," my mother snaps, eyeing me up and down. "And where is your dress? This thing you're wearing is nothing more than a scrap of fabric."

The disdain in her features pushes me over the edge. "We're leaving now. I didn't ask you guys to come visit me, and I'm a college student. I can't just dress like I did at home anymore," I growl, feeling unhinged and angry. My parents bring out the worst in me.

Turning on my heels, I start walking down the stairs.

"Where do you think you're going? If you think we'll let you get away with this, you're poorly mistaken!" my father adds as Hero and I move out of earshot, leaving my parents standing there with their mouths hanging open. I can't even describe the mixture of joy, excitement, and uncertainty that zings through me at standing up to them. I might have won our little standoff, but I doubt this will be the final act.

"You okay?" Hero asks, interrupting the silence between us.

"Yes. I think so." I squeeze his hand still holding mine, just now realizing how glad I am he is with me.

There has always been this fear inside me, every time I've spoken to my parents. Today, I was braver than ever before, and I know exactly why: Hero. I feel protected in his arms and I know he won't let anyone hurt me, especially not my family.

Knowing I need to change the subject, I decide to direct the attention back onto Hero. "Jonathan Miller, huh?" I smile.

"Yep, the most common name in America. That's why nobody called me by my name in prison. There were three other Johns and two more inmate Millers in the unit, plus the guards knew what I was in for, so everybody started calling me Hero, because trying to be a hero was what got me into prison. It just stuck, I guess."

"Well, you were certainly my hero today."

At my words, he gives me a panty melting smile.

Now that I think about it, I don't even know how old Hero is. Or what his favorite color is. I consider asking him these questions, but when I drag my eyes away from him and look where I'm going, I spot Tasha heading in our direction.

She looks between us and wrinkles her nose when she sees us holding hands. "Where are you going with *him*?" she says, like the word leaves a bad taste in her mouth.

I don't really understand why, though.

What's up with her?

"*We* are going to my place," Hero answers for me, annoyance lacing his words. He seems irritated by Tasha's attitude.

Not that I blame him. She's being unreasonably rude, and I don't really like it.

"Seriously?" She raises a brow at me in question.

I don't understand what the problem is. She goes home and out with all kinds of guys. "You shouldn't go home with him, Elyse. He's got a bad reputation, not to mention you deserve better."

My mouth pops open in outrage. I've never seen her act this way before. "Tasha, you don't even know him," I shout. "And you don't get to tell me what to do. You do whatever you want to do with whoever you want, and I don't judge you, so please don't judge me."

She seems taken aback by my harsh words, but I don't really care.

I like Tasha, she has been a good friend to me, but I will not let anyone tell me what to do anymore. I've let my parents control me all my life, and I can't let another person do that.

Hero, obviously pleased by my response, smiles widely.

"I guess if that's what you want. I'm just trying to watch out for you." She frowns.

I feel kind of guilty about being so rude.

"Like you were watching out for her at the party you took her to?" Hero interrupts, scolding her. But it's not like he's lying. Tasha left me and walked off to do her own thing. If he hadn't been there, it could've been bad.

Her eyes roll. "Don't be ridiculous. Nothing happened at that party, except you punching that poor guy."

"Nothing happened, *because* I punched that guy," Hero corrects, anger blazing in his green eyes.

"Whatever. It's not like you're a knight in shining armor. I've heard all about you and the things you've done."

Hero's nostrils flare. "What you heard about me is everyone else's thoughts and opinions. I'm real, as real as it fucking gets, so if you want to ask me something, do it. But I'll tell you flat the fuck out, I will not hurt Elyse the way that bastard tried to the other night."

Tasha doesn't seem taken aback by Hero's clenched fists or darkened gaze.

I know I am. I feel the anxious knot in my belly.

"He didn't hurt her, and I don't believe you, not even a little bit. But since I'm done having this conversation..." She sneers at Hero, then directs her attention back to me. "There's going to be another party tomorrow, and I want you to come. We never get to hangout, and I just kind of miss you," she pouts.

I feel conflicted between them. Tasha, my first friend here, and Hero, the man who has opened my eyes to things. I know I can't make them both happy, so I come up with the best option. "I'll come if Hero comes with me." I smile, trying to ease the tension.

Tasha seems upset by my response, but shrugs. "Okay, whatever you want." Without waiting for Hero's answer, she continues. "I'll see you then." She doesn't even say goodbye, she simply walks past us, heading toward our dorm room.

Hopefully, she doesn't have a run in with my parents on her way up there.

We finish our walk back to Hero's house, and when we get there, I feel like he's too quiet.

"So, are you going to take me to that party tomorrow?"

"If you really want to go, then yes, I'll take you."

"I do. I just want to be a normal college girl, doing what everybody else does. I want the whole experience."

He nods like he understands me. "You want to take a bath?"

I nod and smile at him. A bath sounds amazing right now.

Then he adds, "Together?"

My mouth goes dry, and the smile is wiped off my face in an instant.

He wants us to take a bath together?

"Don't look so shocked. I've seen most of your body naked already. I'd like to see the rest. It's just a bath. I'm not planning on taking your virginity. Unless you beg me again. I don't think I'm strong enough to refuse you a second time."

My cheeks heat up thinking of that night and how I pleaded for him to touch me.

At first, I thought I was only acting that way because of the spiked drink, but the more I thought about it, the clearer the truth became...

I wanted it—I wanted him.

I wanted him to touch me, kiss me, to do things to my body, and let me do things to his body in return. And right now, even through the slight rush of fear, I want nothing more than to take a bath with him.

We go into his place, then walk into the bathroom together, stopping right in front of the tub. Hero turns the water on and puts the plug in the drain while I stand there, awkwardly waiting for him.

When he straightens back up, he takes his shirt off, revealing a muscular chest and toned stomach. Noticing tattoos I hadn't seen before, I reach out to touch the inked skin. Running my fingers over them, I appreciate the way he feels and the way he shudders beneath my touch.

Inching closer, he grabs two hands full of the summer dress I'm wearing and starts pulling it up.

Lifting my arms, I help him get the dress off me quicker. When I'm left in nothing more than my underwear, my heart rate spikes, my cheeks heat, and my entire body starts to feel warm all over.

Hero's pants come off next.

I gulp when I see his very erect penis through the thin fabric of his boxer briefs.

"Look, I told you we don't have to do anything, but that doesn't mean *he* is going to want to stay down." Hero snickers, pointing to his crotch. "But seriously, Elyse, I swear, I won't do anything you don't want me to do."

His words are heartfelt, and I know he's telling the truth. Reaching behind me, I unclasp my bra, wanting to show him I'm not as afraid as I might look. Cool air caresses my exposed breasts as the bra slides off my shoulders down to the floor.

Hero grips the material of his boxers, shoves them down his legs, and steps out of them without even a blink of his eyes.

My mouth waters, and my body quivers with need when I spot his erection. It's so long and thick, and points up to his navel. I catch a glimpse of some shiny metal pierced through the tip and almost gasp. I stop myself from reaching out and touching it.

In horror, I realize I've been staring at it for far too long. My gaze lifts to his amused face, and my cheeks heat. I guess he's noticed as well.

Getting down on one knee in front of me, Hero tugs two fingers into the waistband of my panties and starts to pull them down. His movements are sensual as his knuckles skim my skin all the way down my legs.

Waves of pleasure vibrate through me, and a moan escapes my lips when the sensation becomes too much. All he's doing is touching me and my body is on fire, burning hot as the damn sun.

When he dips his head lower and plants a soft, open-mouthed kiss on my upper thigh only a few inches away from my center, my legs almost give out at the buckle of my knees.

He chuckles and stands to his full height, maneuvering himself into the bathtub. He sinks into the water, his ink covered skin disappearing beneath it.

My teeth sink into my bottom lip as I contemplate my next move.

Hero must feel my wavering because he offers me his hand and says, "Come here. Sit between my legs, your back to my chest."

I swallow around the nervous fear in my throat, then follow his command, stepping into the tub and lowering myself into the hot bathwater. Air hisses from my lungs at the contact of my skin on the water. The water almost burns, but it only takes a few seconds to adjust to it. From behind, he gathers my hair to one side of my neck before easing my back against his chest. Feeling his hard length pushing up against my backside awakens something deep inside me.

I've never felt this craving before, this carnal need for more.

I lean my head back, resting it on his shoulder as he starts nibbling on my neck. His kisses are soft but hungry, his lips almost rough on my skin. I can't think straight with his lips on my skin. His hands come up around my front to massage my breasts, just like he did a week ago. I can feel the throbbing deep inside me.

With two fingers, he rolls my nipple, back and forth, back

and forth. My single moan turns into many, and before I know it, I'm panting, salivating, my head spinning with heady need.

One of his hands leaves my breast and trails down my stomach. My breath hitches in my throat. Every part of my body seems to be on fire. I want his hand to move faster, and without thinking about what may happen, I grab his wrist, pushing his hand beneath the water between my legs.

His husky chuckle is loud in my ear. "You are so eager, so damn reactive to my touch."

I sigh intently as his hand reaches its destination. The second his fingers drag across my clit, I lose it. I arch my back, wanting more, needing more, pushing myself into his hand greedily. My body is overtaken by pure need, so I grab my own breast and start to massage it.

The sensation is unlike anything I've ever experienced before...since I've never actually done this before.

Hero's skilled fingers stay between my legs, drawing little circles over the most sensitive part of me. My walls clench and my pussy throbs with each breath that passes my lips. I can't help but wonder how it would feel to have Hero inside me, stroking me deep from the inside out.

The thought of Hero inside me is what pushes me over the edge. I fall apart into a million little pieces beneath his touch. Every muscle in my body tightens with pleasure before releasing into pure euphoria.

My bones liquefy to molten lava, and I'm floating, completely lifeless, or at least that's what it feels like when I try to move.

"You're so beautiful when you fall apart, so fucking beautiful," Hero whispers in my ear, his teeth nipping at my earlobe, making the pure need spiral out of control deep inside me.

And all over again, I'm left panting with need, for him—for whatever we are.

7

ero

HER BODY IS SO responsive to me and my touch, I nearly come unglued when she grinds her backside against my hardened cock. I have to clench my jaw and pray for the will to keep touching her without giving into my own carnal needs.

"Hero." My name falls from her lips breathlessly.

I know what she needs, wants. The question is, can I give it to her?

She's so pure, so sweet—she's everything a bad man like me should never touch or have, but I'm selfish, this I know, and so I'll have her. I'll keep taking until she doesn't want me anymore.

Taking my hand, she eases it back down between her legs. My thumb circles her clit, and two fingers press against her virgin entrance. I doubt she'll be able to handle anything more than one finger, so I slip just the tip of it inside and nearly growl with need as her walls clench around the thick digit.

"This okay?" I grit out, wanting her to feel nothing but

comfortable and safe in my arms. She nods her head and moves forward, lowering herself onto my finger completely. Water sloshes out the sides of the tub, and I couldn't give a damn. The air sizzles between us. I want to fuck her so bad, it hurts.

My cock is swollen with need, smashed between our two bodies. Every little movement she makes pushes on the fucking muscled beast. He wants her, just as much as I do. Feeling the flutters inside her pussy, I move my finger in and out of her ever so slowly, forcing myself to go slow.

"Oh god…" she whispers, as if she's sinning by the saying the very words.

It makes me smile knowing how dirty and bad I'm going to make her soon. "You going to come again for me? I want to feel your virgin pussy clench around me," I murmur into her ear, then bite hard on the soft flesh.

Her body shakes, and her hands grip onto my arms as if she needs them to hold her to this world. "I-I feel it…"

I can't see her face, but I fucking wish I could. "Your body's tightening, your pussy is squeezing my finger so tight, my cock is jealous. Come for me, baby. Come all over my hand…" Then, as if she's following a direct command, her body shakes against mine, her pussy squeezing me tight, making my cock jealous with every single fucking flutter. God, I'm so envious of that finger right now, I don't even want to look at it.

I want Elyse, and I want her bad. She's not ready, and I know that, so I won't push her. Instead of fucking her like I want, I decide to do something else, something just as good.

"I want to see your face. Turn around and sit in my lap." My cock jumps when she stands on wobbly legs, her face speaking every emotion she's feeling as she turns around in the tub and comes face to face with me. Kneeling with her knees outside mine, she sits her bare pussy against my thighs, my thick member caught between our bodies.

I reach out for her, my hand cupping her warm cheek, my thumb gliding across her plump pink bottom lip. I can see how flustered she is, how consumed with need she is for me.

Her blue eyes sparkle with excitement, her small hand resting against mine. Looking at her now, I know she's gotten beneath my skin. She's inside me, and I'm consumed by her, obsessed with her.

"Do you want me...?" her voice trails off, her eyes dropping to my cock.

Fuck, will I be able to handle that, her hand touching me, jacking me off?

"I'd be lying if I said I didn't want you." My voice cracks, arousal dripping from every single word. *Fuck.*

I trail my hand down her chest, feeling it heave with nervous breaths, her heart hammering against her rib cage.

"W-What do you want me to do?" she asks.

I almost smirk. *So much, baby, so much...* I nearly say it, but instead, I take her hand and guide it to my stiff cock. As soon as her soft hand wraps around my length, I hiss out through my teeth.

Jesus.

"Am I doing this right?" she asks, her eyes alluring as she moves her small hand up and down, up and down. Her grip isn't hard enough for me, and I worry I might hurt her feelings by telling her that, so I wrap my hand around hers beneath the water and pump, every glorious stroke bringing us closer and closer together.

"Fuck, Elyse..." I tighten my grip around her hand, making her stroke me harder and faster. I need more, I need it rough to come, but I don't want to push her too far or scare her off. Taking my chances anyway, I growl, "More. I need it harder."

At my words, a new feeling reflects in her eyes. Lust and the desire to please me are still center stage, but my admission of wanting it rougher has sparked some fear within her.

Even with that fear, she does as I ask and strokes me harder, more ferociously, her hand squeezing me like I wish her pussy could.

My eyes roll to the back of my head as the pleasure of her touch rips through me.

I stroke faster, feeling the water slosh more and more. My grip tightens on hers as I fist my cock within our hands. With her new roughness, she drives me closer to the edge. Heat rolls through my belly as my muscles tighten, working up to the best orgasm I've ever had in my life—at least from a hand job.

I blink my eyes open momentarily and gaze up at her. Her expression cannot be described. Excitement. Curiosity. Love? Love...an emotion I hadn't experienced since my mother. I've never loved anyone but her, and the fact that my obsession with Elyse is turning into something more scares me.

I groan, my orgasm hitting me full force as her sweet lips press against mine. Ropes of sticky cum shoot from my cock into the water. Elyse pulls back with a gasp, realizing I finally came, her eyes going wide. "Did I do good?" Her singsong voice fills my ears.

"Fuck yes you did, baby. I came, didn't I?" I pull my hand away ever so slowly and moan in pleasure as she keeps her hand against me, touching the barbell at the tip of my velvet head.

"I can't wait to be inside you. To claim you." I pull her into my chest, whispering the words against her lips. "You want that, don't you? For me to be your first? To claim you?" If she says no, I don't know what the fuck I'll do. It will kill me.

Thank fuck she nods her head yes, and I don't miss her beautiful pink hardened nipples rubbing against my chest. "I could fuck you now. Slide deep inside you."

She doesn't say anything, so I continue. "My obsession with you runs that deep. I want you and need you always. When I'm awake, when I'm asleep, I want you."

She visibly swallows, moving her hands from my cock and up my body to rest on my shoulders.

Her touch is scorching hot. I want to tell her she owns me, inside and out, but I'm not ready just yet.

"I want you to be my first, Hero." Her voice wobbles. "B-But I'm not ready yet." She sounds sorry, as if she has a reason to be.

"I know, baby. That's why I'm not ten inches deep inside you right now. We go at your pace. Always." I kiss her fiercely, ensuring she knows I mean what I'm saying. When it comes to her, I'll always do what she needs me to. I'll be the good man. I'll protect her, cherish her, and in return, I'll get to keep her as mine.

"Thank you. Thank you for everything—for being there for me today, for waiting…" She sighs, and it sounds heavenly.

"It's all for you, Elyse. All for you."

8

lyse

I KNOW Hero doesn't want to go to the party Tasha invited us to, but I'm determined to be a college student and get the full experience. Plus, it seems to mean so much to her that I hang out with her. My last run in at a party hadn't gone as planned, but I had no fear with Hero being there with me.

"Can I ask what you were doing at the last party?"

"You didn't figure that out yet?" He smiles and tucks some of my hair behind my ear. "I was there for you, obviously."

"Oh." Maybe these things are obvious to a normal girl, but not me. "So, you don't mind coming to the party with me tonight? I need to go back to my dorm and change clothes before we go." I curse myself for not bringing some of my stuff with me. I love being taken care of by Hero, but I also like having my own stuff, like my bathroom products and clothes.

"Sure. We can go over there in a little bit, baby."

I push up onto my tiptoes and give him a peck on the lips.

Instead of leaving it at a quick kiss, he wraps his arms around me, pulling me into his body. I snake my own arms around his neck, intensifying the kiss even further, wanting it to go deeper and further. A phone ringing drags us out of our lust filled haze and a pout forms on my lips because the kiss ends far sooner than I want.

Hero rolls way with a groan, telling me he, too, was hoping it would go for longer. When he pulls out his cell phone, he takes another step back away from me. "I need to get this," he mumbles.

As soon as he looks at the screen again, his face changes. Something is up.

He curses under his breath before he answers. "What's up, man? Are you serious? Wait... Okay, just hold on... The warehouse on twenty-fifth? Got it. Just stay put." He hangs up a second later, slipping the phone into his pocket again. "Sorry, babe. No party tonight. I've got to go somewhere and help out a buddy of mine." His words come out in a rattled rush.

Slipping on his boots, he grabs his keys, and I realize just how big of a hurry he is in to leave. Whatever, or whoever, that was must be important to him.

Feeling disappointed, I decide I'll go instead. "It's okay. I can just go with Tasha."

My words halt his movements. "No, you won't." He looks at me as if he's shocked I would even suggest such a thing. "You will not go to another party without me. No way in fucking hell, Elyse. I cannot protect you if I'm not there."

Flabbergasted, I'm not sure what I should say.

Had he actually asked me to stay here, I may have agreed, but that's not what he's doing. He is trying to order me to stay, and I've spent enough of my life letting people order me around. No way am I going to let him do it too.

Squaring my shoulders and lifting my chin, I look him dead

in the eyes. "I will go and do whatever I want, with whomever I want."

"I don't have time for this," he grumbles, like I'm inconveniencing him.

I'm angry, sad even, and the look on my face must give my emotions away because a second later, he leans into me.

"Look, I'm sorry, but I can't let you go by yourself. It's not happening." The look in his eyes tells me he's serious. The next thing I know, he's lifting me up and throwing me over his shoulder caveman-style.

"What are you doing? Let me down!" I demand, pounding my fists on his back. He carries me down the hall with ease, ignoring my punches and demands. Flopping me down on the bed, I bounce twice before I'm able to get enough control over my own body to sit up.

"What are you doing, Hero?" I ask again, this time louder and slightly panicked, even though I know for certain he heard me the first time I asked.

He looks at me with apologetic eyes, and I almost believe him when he says, "I'm sorry."

Hero doesn't say another word to me. He just turns around and walks to the bedroom door. He gives me one more look and pulls it shut behind him, leaving me sitting on the bed confused and hurt.

What is going on? I can't comprehend why I'm in here.

And then I hear it. The lock on the door clicking into place is like taking a knife to the heart.

He locked me in.

"Hero!" I call out to him, rushing from the bed, nearly tripping over the bed sheets. I slap my hands against the wooden door as tears sting my eyes.

"No, Elyse. I'm sorry. I really fucking am, but I can't risk something happening to you and me not being there. I'd kill someone, even myself, if I let that happen, and I can't do it. I just can't. So please, fucking please, just stay in here until I get back."

The anguish in his voice tells me he's upset about doing this, but that's not enough to me.

I blink away the tears in my eyes. This feels like betrayal of the worst kind. When I hear the front door slam off in the distance, I'm frozen in time. I cannot believe he did this to me!

I have to get out of here and kick his ass. Anger burns inside me. Weak and mindless is what my father always called women—me. I clench my fists and walk into the bathroom connected to the bedroom. I go to the small window above the toilet and eye it curiously, wondering if I could fit through it.

Then I turn and walk back into the bedroom, searching for something, anything, I could use to get me out of here. I stop in front of the door, eyeing it intently, as if it's going to give me all the answers I need.

And then it does.

Pushing against the door, I notice one of the hinges is already loose and the other parts are just tightened up with regular screws. A light bulb goes off inside my head. If I could find something flat and small to use as a screwdriver, I could take them off and escape this room.

I search the room like a madwoman, looking through every drawer and on top of every cabinet. After a few minutes of searching, I end up looking through his nightstand. The first thing that catches my eye is a box of condoms.

My stomach drops. The box is open, and it looks like there might be some missing inside.

Bile rises into my throat at the thought of him with someone else.

Even though I knew I won't be his first, it still hurts to see the evidence at hand. It awakens unpleasant feelings of jealousy in me, and I don't like it. Not even a little bit.

Pushing those feelings down, I go through the rest of the

drawer. A bottle of lotion, lighter, a cell phone charger. Ugh, none of those things will get me out of here. I'm close to ripping my hair out when I spot something shiny in the very back of the drawer. I grab the item and examine it.

Bingo!

It's a folded-up pocket knife.

I take the knife and walk back to the door. Flipping it open, I use the sharp edge to move the screw around, turning it slowly until it falls to the floor in front of me. I repeat with the other screws until all the hinges are loose. With each loose screw, I do a fist bump.

Sliding my fingertips into the small spaces on each side, I grab the door and pull it out of the frame.

I'm so proud of myself, I can't help but smile widely even though no one is here to see it.

Take that, Hero!

My little victory joy is short lived when reality comes crashing back down. He locked me in his room. Not only is that betrayal going to haunt me, I am also left with knowing he just left and didn't tell me why.

What is he hiding from me?

I scrub a hand down my face in frustration. Then I remember the phone call. He said something about a warehouse on twenty-fifth street.

That's where he must be going, therefore I should go there too, since whatever it is he's doing is something he doesn't want to share with me.

A part of me knows I shouldn't follow him. His warnings about how bad he was didn't go unnoticed. Still, the part of me that cares and wants to be her own person decides to follow him, see for myself what he's up to. If there is any chance of me and Hero working out after tonight, I need to know the truth about him—the whole truth.

We can't build a relationship on lies and mistrust. At least, I can't.

I pull on my shoes and grab my phone from the kitchen table. Running across campus, I call Tasha on my way to the dorm. She answers, and I yell into the phone, "I need you to take me somewhere! Please, can you meet me at your car? It's super important."

I'm astonished when she answers the phone, and even more astonished when she agrees. Then again, Tasha being the drama seeker she is would agree without needing any further explanation. "I'll be right there."

By the time I get there, Tasha is already waiting by the car, a pessimistic look on her face. "What's going on?"

"I-I don't know." I don't want to tell her everything that happened since she already hates him enough as it is, but I also need a ride, and Tasha won't do shit without a reason. So, I give her the best, most boring version. "Hero is meeting with someone, and I need to know who and why. So, if you can, I need you to take me to twenty-fifth street. If not, I'll call for an Uber or something." I shake my head. Had he just told me the damn truth, we wouldn't be in this situation.

"Okay, I'll take you. Sounds like some juicy secret ready to be uncovered." She smirks as she gets in and starts the car.

I hop in a second later, feeling all kinds of anxious.

What could he be hiding? Is he meeting with another woman? My thoughts run rampant, and the entire ride over feels like it takes an eternity.

God, the stop signs must have multiplied overnight, and the traffic lights suddenly stay red for hours instead of minutes. My patience starts to wear thin when we finally get to the warehouse.

My mind has conjured up every possible outcome of how this can and will go—most of which all end badly.

I don't know what I'm going to find in there, but considering we are at an abandoned warehouse in a rough neighborhood, I doubt I'll find anything worth finding.

Old warehouses are places where bad things happen, everyone knows that. I mean, no one ever said, 'hey, remember that fun afternoon tea party we had at the abandoned warehouse last week?'

I wipe my hands down the front of my dress and survey the parking lot. Fifty pounds of lead finds its way into my gut the moment I spot Hero's car. I didn't realize it until this very moment, but a part of me kept hoping I wouldn't find him here.

"You can just drop me off here, Tasha," I announce, afraid to even speak.

"Drop you off? Here...?" She shakes her head profusely, her eyes bugging out. "No way! I'm not leaving you here."

"It's okay. Look, Hero is here. He'll give me a ride back."

Tasha glances over at Hero's car like she just caught a bad smell of something. Him being here doesn't ease her mind and probably doesn't make her like him any more than she did before.

"How about a compromise? I'll go in there on my own, and you'll wait out here for me just in case I need you."

Chewing on her lip, she mulls it over. Seconds tick by... "I guess that'll be all right."

I sigh a breath of relief. "You're the best, Tasha." I give her a quick peck on the cheek and rush from the car.

It's nearly dark now, and with no street lights, it becomes harder and harder to see. Every step I take leading up to the entrance adds a few pounds to my gut feeling that something bad is going on inside. Fear of the unknown trickles down my spine.

My hands shake as I slide the heavy metal door open. The sound of the wheels grinding makes me hold my breath. When I don't hear anything, I slip inside and close the door behind me. Cool, musky air greets me, and the dust flying around makes my nose itch.

What the hell could Hero want here?

I walk deeper into the building, my feet moving slowly. It only takes me a few steps before I start hearing voices somewhere off in the distance. Following the noise, I quickly realize there are two voices mixed with groans and cries. My heart rate spikes and the nervousness I felt before is replaced with fear—for Hero.

I pick up speed, each step full of determination. Is he fighting somebody? Is someone hurting him? My thoughts are all over the place.

Running through the warehouse, I weave in between large machinery and things that look like storage containers. When I finally get close enough for the voices to make sense, it hits me.

Hero is yelling at someone, not the other way around. "Tell me where he is!" Hero bellows.

When the other person doesn't answer, a loud smacking noise fills my ears, followed by a grunt.

Confused by what I'm hearing, I keep searching for them, hoping for the best and praying Hero is okay.

"You better tell my friend here what he wants to know. You don't want to see what he is capable of..."

The menace in the unfamiliar voice scares me. There is no way he is talking about Hero, is there?

If you would have asked me ten minutes ago, I would have said no, but when I turn the next corner and Hero comes into view, everything I thought I knew about him changes.

His back is turned to me, but I know it's him, there's no denying it. Images of the way he cares for me, the gentleness of his touch, and the way he smiles down at me. All of those things fade away when I see the man before me.

He's not the same. This I know. Deep in the pit of my belly, I know...this is the part of him he hides.

My body shakes, my feet are cemented to the floor. I know I shouldn't watch, that I should look away, but I can't. Hero looms over a guy tied to a chair. His head is hanging low, his face bloody and bruised. I cover my mouth with my hands, watching the blood trickle down the man's face.

Is he even alive?

Hero's sleeves are rolled up, his hands balled into blood-covered fists. He pulls his arm back, the muscles in his body tense, and hits the poor guy in his stomach full force again and again. One hit, two hits, three hits. Air whooshes from the guy's body, and when blood sputters from his mouth, I whimper, swallowing down the vomit rising into my throat.

In that moment, the guy who appears to be Hero's friend turns in my direction, his eyes homing in on me.

I freeze like a deer caught in headlights, afraid to breathe, blink. I've been caught—and now, they're going to kill me. They're going to do the same thing to me they're doing to him.

"Hey...you!" Hero's friend yells at me.

His voice is so angry, it makes me jump back half a foot. My pulse pounds in my ears when Hero's gaze swings in my direction. All the air leaves my lungs, and my blood turns ice cold when his eyes meet mine. Nothing could have prepared me for what I see when he looks at me.

His eyes are so dark, cold and calculating, they look like they don't even belong to him. I'm paralyzed by fear, and unable to move a single muscle. His lips move, as if he's saying my name, but I can't hear anything.

It isn't until I see him take a step toward me that my body decides to work again. I twist around and start running back the same way I came. My chest heaves as my legs move frantically, wanting to get out of here as fast as possible. I can't breathe, can't think, I just need to leave this place and forget what I saw.

Everything will be better if I forget. Forget the look in his eyes...the blood on his fists. I squeeze my lids closed for half a second, wishing I hadn't seen what I had.

"Elyse!" Hero's voice calls out after me. I can't tell if he's angry, but that only makes my legs stronger and faster, pushing harder to get away from this nightmare—from him.

"Elyse!" he screams my name.

He's getting closer now. I turn my head to look behind me, to see there are only a few feet between us, and he is closing the distance quickly.

Before I can turn my head back around, my foot catches on the side of one of the shipping containers. Everything seems to happen in slow motion.

One moment, I'm running, and the next, I'm tumbling, losing my balance mid run. My other foot lands wrong, and I know right away I'm in trouble. Pain like I've never felt before radiates through my ankle and up my leg.

Out the corner of my eye, I see Hero reach for me, but he's still too far away and his hand grabs thin air.

I fly forward, about to the hit the unforgiving concrete floor when my arms come up by instinct, trying to break my fall. *Bad idea. Bad idea,* I tell myself, but it's too late. My right hand touches the ground before anything else, and I hear the crack before I feel the pain.

The cry that leaves my lips is unlike any sound I've heard myself make before. It scares me, terrifies me straight to the bone. I curl up on the cold, hard floor into the fetal position, holding my wrist to my chest, hoping my outcome isn't the same as the man's back there.

"No...Elyse. Shit, babe..." Hero's hand lands on my shoulder, pulling me toward him.

I jerk away, like his touch burns my skin. Even through the pain, I don't want his bloodied hands on me.

All I can see inside my head is the man slumped over in the chair, blood dripping from his face.

Rolling onto my back, I scoot back on my elbows, trying to get away from him. "D-Don't touch me! Just don't hurt me, and I won't tell anyone. I promise."

The hurt in his eyes is apparent, but it's nothing compared to the hurt I'm feeling. I feel like I just took a bullet through the heart that left me with a gaping wound in my chest.

I try to push myself up onto my feet, but quickly realize I must have twisted my ankle as well. Crying out in pain, I sink back to the floor with a hard thud.

"Baby, please, let me help you." Hero doesn't wait for my answer even as I scurry away from him. Slipping one arm under my legs and the other around my shoulders, he lifts me up and cradles me to his chest.

I try to break free of his hold, but there isn't any point. With a hurt leg and hurt wrist, even if I did get him to let me go, how would I get away? I try to calm my breathing and erratic heartbeat, but nothing helps.

I want to hate him. How can I feel anything besides disgust and hate after what I just witnessed? I'm conflicted...confused...

Yet, when I'm in his arms, so close to him, I feel safe.

Turning my head, I bury my face into his shirt and start crying. I know it doesn't make sense for him to be able to calm me down, since he is the one causing the panic in the first place, but he does.

"It's okay. You're okay. I've got you." Hero continues to whisper sweet nothings in my ear, and I let him.

I let him comfort me, because despite everything, he is the only one who can give me the comfort I need right now. "What...were you doing?" I manage to get out between the sobs wracking my body. I have to know—was he going to kill again? Did that man ask him to? I need answers, and I need them now.

Hero doesn't answer or even look at me at first. All I see is his jaw set in a hard line. He's angry, pissed, but so am I.

"Hero?" I whisper carefully.

"What are you doing here?" he growls, ignoring my question, his arms tightening around my body. "I asked...no, I begged you to stay at home and wait for me." His words make it sound like he is sad, but he isn't. Not really. He's only sad I found out. "Why did you have to come here? Fuck, why, Elyse? I never wanted you to see this."

His grip on me is almost painful, but I don't say a word. There's nothing left for me to say if he won't give me the answers I need.

Feeling more broken than I've ever felt before, I consider the fact that maybe Tasha and my parents were right—maybe Hero isn't really a hero after all.

9

ero

I WANT TO THROTTLE MYSELF. Every sob shaking her small body in my arms sends another shard of glass straight through my heart.

This is all my fault. I knew I should've told Damon to fuck off and deal with his problems on his own. But he's like a brother to me and had my back when I needed it, so I figured I could repay him without getting my hands too dirty.

Ha. It's never that easy, though. I should have known. Why was I so fucking stupid to think otherwise? Now, I will have to live with this mistake for the rest of my life, never being able to forget the way Elyse looked at me. The horror in her gaze made me feel as if I had lost her. She was scared of me, scooting away from me as if I was going to hurt her.

I could feel the turmoil within Elyse. She wants to hate me, to be scared of me, and maybe she should be, but the way she's leaning into me and fisting my shirt in her tiny hands tells me she needs me just as badly as I need her.

I want to tell her I'm sorry, but I can't bring myself to say it yet. I'm too angry with her right now. Angry for coming here, getting hurt, and for making me show her the worst part of me—a part she never should've seen.

I heave the warehouse door open and step outside into the parking lot. The air is cool against my heated skin. I cradle Elyse closer to my chest, as if doing so will change the things she saw or the way she looks at me.

Seeing the pain on Elyse's face, I'm certain I need to take her to the hospital.

With the way she fell onto her hand, I'm pretty sure she's broken her wrist.

"Oh god, it hurts so bad," she whimpers into my shirt.

Fuck, this is all my fault. All my fucking fault.

"I know, baby. I'm taking you to the hospital." And then, it dawns on me. How the hell did she even get here? "Who drove you here?" I barely get the words out before I look up from Elyse's face and spot Tasha's car parked a few hundred feet away. Her car door flings open, and she jumps out, running toward us.

Shit! I don't need her here.

Her brows furrow in confusion, that confusion slowly turning to worry as she gets closer, taking in the situation. "What happened?"

"She fell and twisted her ankle," I say, trying to keep my voice even and calm, but the adrenaline is still coursing through my veins. I feel like losing it, ripping this whole fucking place to pieces. I haven't felt this way since prison, and I don't know how to reel it in—or if I want to.

Tasha comes to a sudden stop a few feet away from us. Her face turns a ghostly white as she catches a glimpse of my hands.

I know what she's thinking, and it's true. I'm a monster. A criminal. A piece of shit.

Then, as if Elyse can tell what's going on, she interjects, "I'm fine, Tasha, really. He is telling the truth. I just fell."

Elyse tries her best to assure her friend, but it's already too late. Tasha is terrified.

I clench my jaw, holding back the words I want to say. I can't deal with her right now. She's my last priority—the last thing I care about in this situation. So, instead of trying to calm her down and explain the situation, I just walk past her toward my car. "You can believe whatever the fuck you want, but I'm taking Elyse to the hospital."

To my surprise, Tasha doesn't say another word. Instead, she follows me to my car, opening the back door for me.

Carefully, I lay Elyse on the backseat, making sure not to touch her wrist or foot. I give her a once over, hating myself even more when I see the tears slipping from her beautiful blue eyes. I never wanted to see her cry, not at my hands, or anyone else's, and here I am, the reason she's hurt.

I swallow down the pain I'm feeling and shut the door before walking around to the driver's side. My hand hovers on the handle when I see Damon running across the parking lot, heading directly for me.

He's giving me a crazy look, like I'm insane or something. "What the fuck are you doing, Hero?"

"She's hurt, so I'm taking her to the hospital." I pull open the door and sink into the driver's seat. I don't care what Damon thinks right now. Nothing he says will change what I need to do for her, my everything.

When I try to pull the door shut, Damon grabs it, halting my movements. "Are you fucking crazy? She saw us. She's a liability, Hero. We need to get rid of her, not take her to a fucking doctor."

Get rid of her? I'm not sure I heard him right, so I play back his words inside my head. Get rid of her? To my people, that means one thing: death.

That's the last word I hear rattle around inside my head before I lose all my senses. My mind goes blank, my body goes numb, and all I see is red. My vision is blurred with fury and rage.

I shove from the car and charge him. There was a time when I couldn't have imagined myself fighting my best friend for any reason, let alone over a girl, but right now, I could kill him, and I just might. How dare he threaten her. Threaten my Elyse. The thought of her hurt any more than she is snaps me in two.

Fuck him. Fuck them all.

There's a flicker of surprise and terror in Damon's dark eyes as my fist connects with his jaw. The impact is so violent, it vibrates through my entire body. I'd be lying if I said I didn't love it. Bones crunching underneath my knuckles is all I feel. I hit him again, and again, not letting him get even a single punch in.

Tasha screams something, but I don't hear a single word. I do, however, feel her hands against my skin, trying to pull me back toward my car, but I'm not done with this fucker...not even close.

"Dude, what the fuck is wrong with you?" Damon staggers, wiping at his bloodied lip and nose.

I point straight at him. "You!" I roar. "You are the problem. Having me come out here. Making me do this shit." I'm losing my mind. My nostrils flare, and my body shakes. I tug at my hair, taking an unsteady step back.

"Me?" Damon huffs. "I didn't make you do shit. You came here of your own free will, and that girl..." He points to my car.

I take a step toward him, ready to throw another fist at his face. Even the slightest mention of Elyse has me unhinged.

"She's going to get you put back in jail, and then what...? What the fuck will you do?"

I shake my head, trying not to listen to him. Elyse is innocent, weak, unknown to the life I live.

She'll never make it. I mean, look at her after just witnessing what she did tonight. Doubt swirls around inside my head.

I'm so angry at her, at myself...at my shit life. I'm obsessed with her, crazy with need for her, but I can't risk hurting her. I can't risk her being involved in any other crazy shit. This ends tonight.

"Do the right thing, Hero..." Damon backpedals, putting more distance between us, his hand wiping at his bloody nose, his eyes still piercing mine. "If you don't, I will. We can't have any loose ends ever, not even her." I force myself to stay where I am.

I want to kill him, rip his heart out, but part of me knows he's right. She's a liability I cannot afford, and I don't want to go to prison again. She's ruined us—ruined it all.

Damon disappears back into the warehouse.

I can hear Tasha sobbing behind me. When I turn around, I see her hand over her mouth, fear spiking in her eyes. Good, she should be afraid, real fucking afraid. I separate the space between us in a second, my eyes bleeding into hers.

I don't want to have to hurt Tasha, but I have to do whatever I can to protect myself...and since she doesn't care about anyone but Elyse, I know exactly what I must do.

"Tell anyone what you saw here tonight, and I will hurt her," I sneer, though my heart feels as if it's bleeding as I say the words. "Anyone...the cops, a friend, your boyfriend, your grandma—anyone finds out, and I'll destroy her." I force myself to smile, making sure she understands how serious I am. "Do you understand?" I growl.

Tasha nods her head furiously. She looks like she might puke, but I don't care.

I don't fucking care about anyone. I'm broken, twisted, fucked up, and nothing and no one is ever going to change it.

If anything—tonight showed me that.

10

lyse

TEARS STAIN my cheeks and I force myself to breathe. In. Out. In. Out. But the panic attack claims me. I'm numb, hanging off the edge of a cliff, seconds away from falling into the unknown.

My heart is pounding so hard, I feel like I'm on the verge of a heart attack. My eyes are squeezed shut so tightly, I'm afraid to even open them. When I hear the squeaking of the car door and strong arms pick me up out of the backseat, they finally flutter open.

Hero's holding me, carrying me. I look up into his eyes, begging, pleading to see that man, the one I know cares for me.

"Hero...what's happening?" I croak, my voice weak. He doesn't answer me, though. In fact, his body is so tense, his anger vibrates off him, slamming into me.

I wish he would talk to me, say something, anything. I open my mouth to ask again, but the words freeze on my lips when he stops walking. His eyes stay trained ahead. Another car door opens, and he places me inside it. My gaze swings around, and I realize I'm now in Tasha's car.

"What's...what's going on?" I'm in full blown panic mode. He told me he would take care of me, that he'd protect me no matter what.

"Take her to the hospital or back to the dorms. Whatever the fuck you want to do, but remember..." Hero's voice is vacant of any emotion and a warning hangs in the air between them. I peer through the window, pounding on the glass with my good hand. Tasha visibly gulps, her eyes wide and full of fear.

Hero leans into her face. "Remember, you do anything stupid, she gets it."

Something inside me snaps, breaking in two. All I know now is the Hero I knew, the Hero I cared for, is gone.

Tasha nods her head in understanding.

Hero dismisses her, turning around on his feet and walking back in the direction of his car.

I sag against the seat, my heart broken, fear, confusion, and sadness threatening to drown me.

Tasha enters the car slowly, her hands shaking as she closes the door and buckles her seatbelt.

She's scared. It's written all over her face.

"We—I-I need to get you to the hospital." Her voice sounds calm.

I can't even feel the pain from my wrist or ankle any longer. It's just a dull ache in comparison to the pain I'm feeling inside my chest. "He won't hurt me, Tasha," I reassure her, holding my wrist to my chest. I feel betrayed, broken, lost, and damaged. I trusted him—and I was so stupid to do so, because now I'm here, and he's gone.

"He will, Elyse. He will. I saw the look in his eyes. I mean, he already has. Look at you. Look at me." She sounds so unstable, so afraid.

Taking in her words, I swallow them down and consider

that maybe she is right...maybe she was right all along. Her warning isn't for nothing, and it's painfully obvious now.

Still, pieces of me cling to the Hero I knew, the man beneath the mask. I may not be experienced in much of anything, but I know pain, and Hero is hiding his, shoving it way down deep.

Tasha doesn't say anything more to me and starts driving.

The pain in my wrist is nothing more than a dull ache now, and I decide I'm better off nursing the damn wound myself. If I go to the hospital, my parents will find out, and if they find out, they'll try to get me to come back with them.

It's not something I can afford to deal with right now. The last thing I need is another run in with them. "Let's go back to the dorms."

Tasha looks at me through the rearview mirror. "What? Your wrist is clearly broken, and Hero had to carry you out of there. Aren't you worried you've hurt something?" Her response is typical Tasha.

I shake my head.

"I *know* I hurt something, but I can't go to the hospital." I frown. "If I do, my parents will find out, and if they find out, that's another storm I have to endure. I've broken plenty of bones before. There isn't anything a doctor can do I can't do myself." And that's the truth, at least when it comes to broken bones. "We'll just get a brace, I'll wear that for a few weeks, and before you know it, I'll be better than new." I force myself to smile.

Tasha doesn't seem like she wants to listen to me, but as we get closer to town, she heads in the direction of the dorms instead of the hospital.

I damn near sigh in relief.

When we pull into the parking lot of our building, she puts the car in park and kills the engine. Then she turns in her seat to face me. "We need to go to the police...you know that, right?"

"No!" The word comes out in a scream, and I slowly exhale,

calming my voice before I continue. "We can't go to the police for the same reason we can't go to the hospital. Don't you get it?" I plead with her to understand and hope she buys this is the only reason I don't want to go to the police. Because the truth is, I wouldn't do that to Hero. He might be able to hurt me emotionally, but I will not inflict the same pain on him. Not when I know he does really care about me, deep down inside.

He might've messed up tonight, but that doesn't mean he deserves to go back to prison, and even if it did, it doesn't mean I want to be the reason he goes back.

"Okay," she whispers, her voice soft. She's not acting like herself at all, but then again, neither am I. There is no taking back what we saw tonight, or the things that were said.

"It's going to be okay, Tasha." I lean forward and give her a half hug, wanting to put all our broken pieces back together.

But even I know the broken pieces of my heart will never be whole again. Not until I see him. Not until I get the answers I need.

THE NEXT WEEK goes by in a blur. My wrist is healing up nicely in the brace Tasha picked up from Walgreens. I focus on my studies as best I can and hope every day he'll show up at my door to apologize. I make sure my phone is charged and the volume is up just in case he finally returns any of my calls or texts.

So far, he's done neither, and with each passing day, I'm getting more and more impatient. I know this entire thing is my fault, but I still feel like he should have come to his senses by now.

Tasha thinks I'm crazy for trying to get in touch with him at all, but I ignore her warnings. I know him. I know he didn't mean the things he said to her that day.

I walk across campus, my feet dragging the entire way. Today is Thursday: paid study session day. Even though I'm glad I didn't officially quit my job, like Hero had suggested, I haven't been looking forward to today either.

My heart beats frantically against my ribcage, as if it's trying to break free and fly away. Each step I take up the stairs and into the library makes it beat faster, harder.

Then, I feel it. A slight change in the air. Just like in the past few days, I have this feeling someone is watching me. I narrow my eyes and turn around, scanning my surroundings.

Has he been watching me?

He admitted to watching me before, so it must have been him. Who else would be sneaking around after me? Or maybe I'm just being paranoid hoping he's watching me, hoping he's sorry. Righting myself, I straighten my back and hold my head high.

Today, he'll finally have to come face to face with me, and I'll demand answers—answers I deserve.

When I get to the study room, I pause in front of the door with my hand on the knob. Is this it? Will he already be inside waiting for me? I take a calming breath to brace myself for the onslaught of emotions surely awaiting me.

The knob turns, and I push open the door, revealing an empty room. Disappointment washes over me like a tidal wave, pulling me down deep into the water.

Ugh, he isn't here yet.

I walk inside the room and slump down into one of the chairs—the same chair I sat in when I kissed him for the first time. The memory of that day brings tears to my eyes. I was shocked when he made that request, but I had never been so excited, or felt so alive. Kissing him was one of the most exhilarating experiences of my life, and it didn't help that he was my first kiss either. I will never forget the way my body reacted to him, or the way it continued to react to him.

I bring my fingertips to my lips, as if I could still feel the kiss there. But the warmth is gone, and so is the taste. I need to see him. I need to have him back.

Checking my phone, I realize it's already ten after six. If he were going to show up, he'd be here by now. Slinging my backpack over my shoulder, I stomp out of the study room far more determined than I've ever expected myself to be.

I'm done waiting for him to come around. I don't care what he thinks is right for me. I want answers, and I want them now.

In the time it takes me to walk to his place, I let every possible scenario run through my head. Maybe he'll open the door...just to slam it in my face again. Or maybe he isn't there at all, or maybe he'll just pretend not to be there.

The worst case scenario would be another girl opening the door. I don't know if I would survive that one, but I guess I'm about to find out.

By the time I get to his apartment, my still sore ankle is throbbing. I concentrate on the pain to keep me grounded.

Lifting my good hand, I beat against the heavy wooden door. My heart races at hummingbird speed as I listen intently for any noise. *It's now or never...right?*

When I finally hear footsteps approaching, I think I might just pass out from anticipation alone.

The door swings open, revealing a freshly showered Hero, wearing nothing but a pair of low hanging shorts.

Looking him up and down, I feel all the saliva suddenly disappear from my mouth. He looks like my beautiful dark knight. I want to press up onto my tip toes and kiss him. Spill all the words from my lips I've been begging to tell him for the last week, but it's like some kind of silly magic trick is taking place, leaving any words I want to say behind and my tongue drier than the Sahara Desert.

"What are you doing here?" he growls.

The harshness of his voice is like a slap to the face, dragging me back to reality. His eyes are a dark green, and they pierce mine with a cold stare that settles deep into my bones.

"I-I want some answers," I demand...or try to. The man is so intimidating, he makes it hard to say anything when he's looking at me the way he is right now. "I deserve some and you—you know you owe them to me."

Rather than open his mouth to give me the answers like a normal person, he steps forward, grabs me by both shoulders, and pulls me into his apartment. He closes the door behind us, locking the dead bolt into place. Suddenly, I feel like I'm caught in a cage with a wild animal rather than a human.

Before I can get a word out, not that I could get a word out anyway, he's in front of me. His face is so close to mine, I can feel his hot breath on my skin. His body takes up all the light in the room, covering me in shadows.

I part my lips slightly, inviting him to kiss me, hoping, praying he does.

Instead, his hand slithers out, his fingers curling into the back of my neck.

My pulse pounds furiously in my ears. When he releases me, I almost sigh, but my relief is short lived, because he grabs a fist full of my hair and tilts my head back until I have to look up into his eyes. My scalp is on fire as he pulls on the roots, forcing me to keep my eyes on him.

"Is this what you want? The answers you came to find?" His voice is dripping with venom as he lowers his head to my neck, grazing the tender skin next to my ear with his teeth.

My whole body aflame, every inch of my skin electrified. This isn't Hero.

This is the man he warned me about—the man he told me he really was.

His free hand starts roaming my body, down my throat, over my breast, and trailing down my belly. It only takes a second of him touching me for my mind to go blank.

"Did you come because you want this?" He grabs my uninjured hand and brings it to the iron shaft between his legs.

I wrap my hand around him through the thin material of his shorts, and he groans. I want to squeeze harder, give him more pleasure, but I stop myself and pull my hand away. I can't give into him like this. I need to keep a clear head and get what I really came here for.

That's easier said than done, though. Before I can open my mouth, Hero leans into me, pressing his kissable lips harshly against mine, swallowing any of my words and pushing all my brain cells out the window.

Then it occurs to me...

What if this is the only way I can get to him?

If this is what he needs from me right now, I'll give it to him. I'll give him myself.

11

Hero

I WRAP my hands around her tiny waist and push her toward my bedroom. Part of me wants her to stop me, push me away and run out the door as fast as she can. The other part is terrified she might do just that. Then again, I'm not sure I'd let her. I warned her, told her not to come here, yet here she stands in all her glory.

Demanding answers, acting like she can trust me.

Didn't she learn anything?

She's asking for things I can't give her right now, maybe never. She knows I'm not a good man and I've done bad things, yet here she stands.

But at the same time, I've missed her so fucking much. I've missed how soft her skin feels, the honey taste that lingers on my lips when I kiss her, and the way her hair smells, like sunshine and flowers on a summer afternoon.

She's life, and I want to breathe her in, every single fucking molecule of her.

I bury my face into the crook of her neck and inhale her unique scent. It tickles the inside of my nose and does crazy things to my head. She rests her hands on my shoulders as I walk her backwards all the way up to my bed.

Her wrist is now in a brace, and it takes everything inside me not to ask her if she's okay. Leaving her that night killed me. It ripped me apart. But it's for the best—all of this is for the best.

So, I'll give her this. I might not be able to give her answers, but I can give her something else—something she wants just as much as answers, or at least something her body wants.

"What were you doing that night?" She sounds breathless.

I clear my face of any emotions. I can't let her know what I'm thinking, or how having her this close makes me feel. "Let me ask you something, Elyse, why did you come here today? It wasn't just to ask questions." I grin down at her as we reach the bed. The backs of her legs hit it, forcing her to sit down. I'm not sure I can go through with fucking her. I don't trust myself with her, not physically at least.

She gives me a puzzled expression. "What do you mean? Of course it was to ask questions. What else would I come here for?"

I push her gently against the shoulder, but she doesn't budge. In fact, her eyes stay glued to mine. *Fuck!* It's clear she wants to play hard to get with me, and that only magnifies my darker, more primal needs. I know I'm fucked up. I've seen what killing someone can do to you firsthand, but Elyse...she's sweet, pure. She's everything that should stay the fuck away from me, yet I want her. Dammit, I want her more than I've ever wanted anything.

"Okay, you want to play hard to get?" I sneer, and all the blood in my body seems to pump straight to my cock at her wide-eyed, fearful expression. A week ago, I would've hated seeing her look at me like that, but now…it's something I need her to do. It's the boundary I need to keep my heart in line and my head where it needs to be.

"No…" She shakes her head in confusion. Those soft brown locks of hers escape from behind her ear, leaving me with an itch to put them back into place. "I mean, yes…" Her cheeks turn a soft shade of pink. "I didn't come here for sex, Hero. I came here to talk about what happened. About what you were doing that night."

"If you aren't here to give me that pretty pussy, then you aren't here for shit." I lean into her face, making it clear I want something I know she isn't ready to give. That'll get her to run.

I take a step back and cross my arms over my chest, smirking down at her like the asshole I am.

She looks broken, sad, then her features change…

"You don't get to do that, Hero." She shoves from the bed and gets right in my face, rage painting her adorable features.

I have to force myself not to reach out and touch her, because fuck, do I want to touch her. Her tiny fingers press against my bare chest, sending electric shock waves through me.

"I will not be bullied! I will not let you hide behind some mask of fury."

Her words are meant to chip away at my mask, the one she knows I'm wearing. But what she doesn't realize is I'm a master at wearing a mask. Not because I want to be, but because I had to be. I'm stronger, and I'm way fucking better at lying.

I grip her by the wrist firmly, not hard, because truthfully, I want to scare her away, not hurt her. "If you don't want me to fuck you, you better turn the fuck around and walk your ass out of my house. I don't want to talk to you about what could've been. You fucked that up when you didn't listen to me. You did this, not me."

Elyse gives me a doleful expression.

I feel the same emotions she's showing me, just way down deep inside, buried beneath the pain, beneath the sorrow. The question still lingers. Why the fuck didn't she just stay here?

Her tongue darts out over her plump bottom lip.

I wonder what she's going to do next. She shocks the hell out of me when she pulls her hand from my grip and starts undressing. She pulls her shirt off with ease, but her yoga pants are another story. With one working hand, she struggles to pull them down her hips.

I smile smugly, watching her struggle, but deep down in my stomach, I know I won't be able to follow through on my word.

With pink cheeks, Elyse looks up at me, a shyness in her eyes. "I..." she stutters. "I can't get them off." She makes another effort to push them down, seeing as I make no move to help her, but loses her balance halfway through.

I reach out, balancing her without thought, her hot bare skin igniting a fire in my belly. "Are you sure this is what you want? Just mindless sex?"

I watch her visibly swallow, a meek "yes" slips from her lips.

"I won't be gentle with you. I won't cuddle you afterwards. I won't call you. And I won't give a fuck if you come," I say the words through clenched teeth, wanting to stab myself in the heart.

"I know," she whispers, her eyes sad.

Fucking Christ! She's testing me. She has to be.

I pick her up and throw her onto the bed, peeling her yoga pants the rest of the way off. My mouth waters when I see her cute lace panties. Her chest heaves with every breath she takes, and I feel like such a bastard for doing this to her.

"Roll over," I order, but she shakes her head no, a defiance in her eyes that has me on the verge of breaking.

"Fine," I growl, then flip her over onto her belly with ease.

She doesn't fight me, and I hate it. I fucking hate it.

It's time to scare her, to send her packing. Pushing my shorts down to the floor, I lean over her on the bed. I grip her by the hips, forcing her onto her knees.

I rock against her ass and watch as she falls helplessly against the mattress, clearly not ready for what I'm going to give her. With her face pressed firmly into the sheets and her ass in the air, I grip her panties and shift them to one side, exposing her perfectly pink pussy. A gasp escapes her lips, and I fist my cock in my hand, bringing it to her entrance.

"You sure this is what you want? You want me to fuck you?" I barely get the words out. My chest heaves as I try and get oxygen into it. My heart is pounding so hard inside my chest, it feels like I might die. And damn, wouldn't this be a way to go.

"I don't—I don't want it like this, but I want you," she mumbles into the sheets.

She's giving herself to me, but why? So I can break her, hurt her?

"Well, I don't give a fuck what you want." My words are coated in rage as I push my swollen cock against her entrance. The head barely slips inside, and she cries out, but not in pleasure. No, this is a cry of pain.

My grip is tight on her hips, and I exhale, trying to determine my next move. Do I follow through and fuck her like this for the first time, knowing damn well she's a virgin or do I do right by her and give her the best time of her life.

"I'm not scared of you, Hero." Her voice is trembling, giving her away.

Now, I know exactly what I need to do.

I lean forward and whisper into her ear, "You should be..."

12

lyse

I bite my bottom lip and pray he can't see through my very thin vale of lies. I'm so afraid, my body starts to shake. I want this with Hero, but not like this. I want the man who cherished me, promised never to never hurt me. I want him...

"Please don't hurt me," I whisper, wondering if he can even hear what I just said. I told him I wasn't afraid of him, but I am —he's thick, too thick, and I...

The pressure of his body against my backside is lifted, and I'm shocked when his booming voice enters my ears.

"Out. Get the fuck out now!" he roars, causing me to scamper across the bed. I chance a glance up at him and see the anger in his eyes, but it's also mixed with something else. Sadness. Desire. Emotions I am quite familiar with by now.

It takes me a moment, but I swallow my fear down and crawl across the bed, reaching out for his length. It's thick, and throbbing, and completely angry looking, just like its owner.

"What are you doing? You just told me not to hurt you and now you come before me on your damn knees, your tiny hands wrapped around my cock, practically begging me to fuck you." His words are laced with no humor, but the wicked grin on his face confuses me.

"You won't hurt me, Hero. You won't. I know it deep down inside my heart."

A hiss escapes his lips, and his eyes drift closed as I squeeze his member, moving up and down his length. My thumb scrapes over the velvety soft head, and I swear his body trembles.

"And why is that?" His hand wraps around the back of my neck and he massages the aching muscles.

"Because it'd kill you to hurt me. It would be like you hurting yourself."

His movements halt, and he pulls away. His eyes are open now, shining brightly, the green in them drawing me in.

"You're a good liar, but there are some things even you can't hide." I cup his cheek with my free hand as much as the brace allows and watch his eyes soften for a few seconds, proving I am exactly right.

The moment doesn't last long, though. The mask he wears so proudly is carefully put back into place, covering the real man beneath. In an instant, he's grabbing me by the arms below my wrists and pushing me back onto the bed, forcing me to lie flat.

I look up at him and see nothing but a mask of emotions.

He releases his hold on my arms and trails his hands down my body, coming to rest against the hem of my panties. With one hard tug, he rips them right off, causing me to gasp out in shock.

I'm just beginning to digest the fact that I had my panties ripped off when he drops to his knees before me, his head ducking in between my legs, his tongue slipping between my folds, giving me one hard lick.

"I'm going to give you the answers you seek, baby...and you're going to give me this pretty virgin pussy."

I can't even form a thought, let alone speak a single word. Hero is being crude and cold, but he's not hurting me...not really. Both of his hands are on my thighs, spreading me wide. I feel so exposed and at his mercy. His fingers dig into my flesh so harshly, it almost hurts.

His lips close around my clit, and the feelings that surge through me are like pure magic. When he starts to suck, the pleasure becomes borderline painful. My legs try to close automatically, as if they want to ease the build on their own, but his grip on me is forceful and unyielding.

I cry out in pleasure, the sensations overtaking my body like a storm.

My hands grip the sheets around me like they could offer me some kind of help, protection. He'd made me orgasm once before, but this feels different. This feeling is so much more intense, dark, and it scares me.

I can barely breathe as he works my clit relentlessly with brutal force. He's owning me, showing me what he can do to me, and for a second, I fear I might break in half. My body wants to arch off the bed, but the iron grip he has on my legs won't let me budge.

"Hero..." His name falls from my lips like a prayer. "Please," I beg him, not knowing what I'm really begging for.

More? Less? I have no idea.

My brain seems to have checked out and my body now has a mind of its own. Every fiber is functioning on pure primal need, and I don't think I ever want to return to sanity. I thrash back and forth, as if I'm trying to outrun the pleasure spiking through me.

I feel the build, my body cresting, as if I'm a surfer riding a wave. I'm close, so close—I'm just about to tip over the edge and come apart under his tongue when he pulls away, leaving me gasping for air and wanting more. "No..." I whimper, near tears.

"I can taste how much you want my cock," he growls, moving up along my body.

If my whole begin wasn't on fire already, I might have blushed at his crude words. The way his eyes burn into mine has me squirming beneath him. I feel intimidated by him, and maybe that's just because of his huge size.

He leans over me, watching me intently, his fingers trailing over my belly, going lower and lower, until I feel two of his thick digits ghost against my soaked entrance. I consider begging him...for a release, for his touch.

He magically reads my mind and slips them deep inside me. The smirk he gives me sends tingles of pleasure down my spine, and when he finally starts moving his fingers, I feel as if I'm already ready to combust.

In. Out. In. Out. I can hear how wet I am, and it's such an erotic sound. My chest heaves, and heat blooms deep in my belly when his fingers scissor. "Oh god..." I curl my fingers into the sheets.

"This is what you wanted, baby...isn't it?" he whispers, nipping at my earlobe.

My pussy tightens around his fingers. I feel him stretching me, pushing my walls apart.

I quiver with need, my mind reeling. I've never felt such need before. I feel like Hero's a drug and I've taken a hit for the first time.

When he adds a third finger, I nearly lose it. My body shakes, and my hips lift off the bed with the force of the orgasm as it rips through me.

A blinding light appears behind my eyes.

The pleasure ignites a spark inside me.

Withdrawing his fingers, I blink my eyes open and stare up at him as he moves above me.

This is it. I'm about to lose my virginity.

"Last chance, princess," he coaxes. "Last chance to tell me to stop…" His mouth comes up to mine, touching my lips, just barely. His tongue darts out over my bottom lip, begging for entry into my mouth.

I open for him, letting him in. I taste myself on him, and it's something I've never experienced before. "I want you," the words come out breathlessly, but that doesn't make them any less powerful.

The green in his eyes fades to the darkest green I've ever seen.

Using one of his knees to push my legs farther apart, I wonder how this is going to work. With my legs open, a surge of panic shoots through me, and then I feel the soft tip of his dick probe my entrance.

"This is going to hurt before it starts feeling good."

A part of me feels like he might be saying this so I'll ask him to stop. He wants to scare me away, push me out the door, but just hearing his voice takes away some of the panic and fear. "I want you," I repeat, even softer than before, my eyes bleeding into his. A moment of silence settles between us as he leans over me on his forearms, his toned stomach almost touching mine.

He's chaos, and I'm just a girl falling helplessly in love.

"Just remember, you asked for this," he grunts, his fists clenched into the sheets beside my head.

I go to say something, anything, but the words never come. Before I can even take my next breath, he's pushing inside me, filling me with one hard thrust.

The pain is blinding, searing me to the bone. My hands fly up to grip his shoulders, my nails digging into his flesh as I cry out in pain. Feeling impossibly full, I try to breathe through the pain and adjust to his size. Tears spring from my eyes and slide down my cheeks.

Hero stills for a moment before he starts moving again in slow, deeply penetrating motions.

"Hero," I whimper.

"Shhh...it's okay." His lips find mine once more in an all-consuming kiss. A kiss that tells me more than he ever could say out loud. He might have tried to scare me off with his words, but he can't hide behind this kiss.

He bares his soul to me—and I give him mine in return.

With my mind occupied and my body wound tightly with need, the pain between my legs lessens, each stroke bringing more pleasure.

My hands roam free over Hero's back, shoulders, and arms. I want to touch all of him, feel every inch of his body, map him out, memorize him. Moving on top of me, he snatches my healthy wrist and pins it next to my head.

He's gentler with the other side, putting his arm across my elbow to keep my hand from touching him the way I want to. With me immobilized beneath him, he starts moving faster, more viciously. His hips thrust upward, driving into me over and over again, moving me against the sheets.

"You happy now?" Hero pants directly in my ear. "You happy I'm fucking you?" His voice is raw and full of emotion. "You like me deep inside you?"

"Yes..." I'm able to get out in between moans and the slaps of his flesh against mine.

Upon my words, Hero picks up speed, pounding into me over and over again. This time, he twists his hips, sending little rivulets of pleasure straight to my clit.

I can't feel anything but the way he makes my body sing as he pushes me higher and higher. When I finally reach that mountain top, the orgasm hits me so hard, I see stars. I've never felt anything so intense. My entire body spasms and releases, waves of pleasure washing over me, leaving me stranded on a cloud floating into the sky.

But Hero doesn't stop. He grunts and keeps pumping into me, dragging out the aftershock of the orgasm.

Suddenly, he sits up and pulls out of me, and I nearly cry out at the loss of him. I'm mesmerized as he takes his hard length into his fist and begins jerking himself off violently. Instantly, I'm reminded of the time I did it for him. My gaze trails up his perfectly sculpted body as I watch him intently through hooded eyes.

His own eyes are closed, nostrils flared, and a sheen of sweat covers his handsome face. His head falls back while his body jerks with a loud groan. Seconds later, his hot cum lands against my lower belly. And it feels like he is marking me, claiming me.

He keeps pumping himself until he empties every drop onto my skin. He stares down at it like he's deep in thought for a moment, then he gets off the bed without making eye contact.

With my brain still flushed with endorphins and my bones having liquefied under my skin, I do the only thing I am able to right now: I lie here.

Hero disappears into the bathroom, and I hear the water running, then he reappears holding a washcloth. Stopping in front of the bed, he kneels between my legs and cleans me.

My entire body is sensitive, and I shiver at the contact of the scratchy wash cloth against my flesh. When he pulls it away, I see a smear of red. He doesn't lift his gaze to mine. Instead, he gently wipes away his sticky release from my belly.

My stomach twists into knots as I realize I've done exactly what my parents never wanted me to do. I'd broken the most sacred rule in my family's home.

Sex before marriage. And worse yet: without a condom.

I feel stupid and used.

"You're going to be a little sore for a while. If I were you, I wouldn't go around campus fucking any other guys right away. Give it a couple days or you might regret it."

His words hit me like a ton of bricks. They're menacing, cold, and don't fit his caring actions.

"We didn't use a condom," I blurt out, and my cheeks heat when I see Hero's gaze. There's a smug look on his face. I'm not sure if he means it or is doing it to be an asshole.

I know he warned me before, but I thought maybe once we shared this, things would be different again. I thought this made him see we are right for each other. That I can be what he needs me to be.

"Yeah, I know. I pulled out," he states, matter of fact.

"I'm not on birth control," I announce, pushing up onto my elbows. Suddenly, what we've done hits me. I don't know a lot about sex, like nothing at all, but I do know when you do it enough it makes babies.

Hero shrugs and starts walking away. "If you get pregnant, we'll deal with it."

I blink. What does he mean *deal* with it? Something snaps inside me. I'm not sure if it's my emotions spiraling out of control or the sadness of it all, but I have to say something, anything. "How can you say that? Then act like this toward me, even more so since I know you've been watching me."

This gets his attention. Turning, he looks at me over his shoulder.

"I know you still care about me, that's why you've been watching me, isn't it? You've missed me too, haven't you?" I refuse to let him lie to me, not about this.

His eyebrows draw together in frustration. "What the hell are you talking about?"

I drop my gaze. "I feel your eyes on me when I'm walking across campus. I know you've been following me. You don't have to hide it."

Hero shakes his head in disbelief, a ragged exhale leaving

his lips, "Elyse, I've been staying away from you. In fact, I've gone out of my way so I wouldn't run into you. I don't miss you. I don't care about you. You're nothing to me—nothing but a tight hole to fuck."

His words are so hateful, so mean, he might as well have punched me in the face. I would have much rather gotten punched in the face than listen to another degrading word fall from his lips.

"Maybe I'm crazy for believing you had a heart. I must have imagined it—imagined all of this. I guess you don't really live up to your name, do you, *Hero*? I'm sorry for wasting your time." Tears sting my eyes.

I thought this would change things—giving myself to him would make him want me more, but it's apparent now that isn't the case. Hero's lost, and I don't know if I'm willing to jump into darker waters to be with him.

I shove off the bed, ignoring the soreness between my legs, and concentrate on the pain in my chest instead. Gathering my pants off the floor, I pull them over my wobbly legs with shaking hands, surprising myself that I'm able to keep my balance.

My eyes burn with held back tears, but I refuse to give him the satisfaction and cry in front of him.

Out the corner of my eye, I can see him still standing in the same spot, watching me struggle to put my clothes back on. It kills me to know he's still in there, hiding somewhere. I miss him. I miss him so much.

He startles me, his voice booming through the room. "Do you really think someone is watching you?"

"If it's not you, who else could it possibly be? And even if someone else were following me, what do you care? You don't give a fuck about me. I'm just another girl to fuck, right?" I mock him. Cussing seems like one of my lesser wrongdoings today. In fact, I may start doing it more.

With my bra in place, I pull on my shirt and start heading toward the door.

Hero steps in front of me so quickly, I run into his still bare chest. He grabs my elbows, steadying me.

I look up at him in surprise.

"You are staying here," he orders, pushing me backwards, back to the bed where I just came from.

"W-What?"

"You heard me. You are staying here." He deposits me back onto the bed and turns on his heels, walking toward the door. He had his boxers on now, but it doesn't stop my eyes from dropping to his ass.

"What?" I repeat, much louder and more demanding than the first time.

"You can sleep in my bed, I'll take the couch. If you think someone is watching you, it's not safe for you out there on your own. Until we know what's going on, you'll stay here at least until I'm sure no one is trying to kill you."

"Kill me?" I shriek.

Hero looks at me like he knows something I don't, and that scares me. All of this does.

"Yes, kill you, as in dead, died, gone," he draws out the words, making a different kind of shiver run down my spine.

And just like that, Hero's mask slips out of place, and I feel like there might be a chance for us after all.

13

ero

Looking down at the small frame of her shaking body evokes a whole new set of feelings inside me. I've been mean, carless, and hateful—all to protect her from my past, from the person I really am. But at what cost?

Her feelings, our future...

She continues to shake as I pick up the blanket and cradle her in my arms, whispering promises I know I can't keep.

"You'll always be safe with me and I'll never hurt you again."

What the fuck am I supposed to do now?

Everything I've done is to protect her, but how can I protect her if someone is after her? It could be a ploy I suppose, but Elyse is innocent, and she'd never be cunning enough to come up with something like that, especially if she thought it's been me watching her.

"*We need to get rid of her.*" Damon's words ring in my ear.

That fucker. It has to be him. Who else could it be? I play the rest of his words back in my mind.

"Because if you don't, I will. We can't have any loose ends ever, not even her." He basically told me he would come after her. I thought my fist to his face gave him a clear enough message, but apparently fucking not.

I tighten my hold on Elyse and press my nose into her golden-brown hair. Her scent calms me and warms me all over. I've missed her—so fucking much, it hurts. I don't know how I've survived the last few days without her. My thoughts are a jumbled mess, but the only thing I can think about is how horrible I was to her tonight.

I take in one more deep breath, sucking in as much of her unique scent as I can.

"Do you really mean it?" She sniffles into my chest, her body resting on mine.

"Mean what?" I shift her in my arms so I can look into her eyes. There are tears forming, close to spilling over the rims. Knowing I'm the one making her cry tears me apart.

I want to punch myself in the face for doing this to her, she deserves better, so much fucking better.

"Everything. Did you really not miss me? Because being without you killed me. I waited for a text or call, anything. I was upset and paranoid and thought if only I could catch you watching me, maybe I could confront you."

The anguish in her voice slices me in half. I want to tell her everything, but I can't lie to her anymore tonight. Not that it really matters. I'll lie to her again. I can't tell her the truth. Not when it's for the better.

"I'm going to sleep on the couch. In the morning, we're going to see Damon and put an end to this. Then you'll be safe again and can go back to your own place."

The tears finally spillover, finding their way down her perfect little face.

Fighting the urge to touch the shiny path the tears have left behind, I step back, putting some distance between us.

I have to force myself to leave the room and close the door behind me. Each step away from her kills me, but I can't be close to her and not touch her, not right now. Walking into the kitchen, I head for the sink. I turn on the faucet and splash some cold water onto my face, hoping it wakes me up from this nightmare.

What the fuck did I do?

I fucked up, that's what I did. Meandering over to the fridge, I open it and grab a beer out. I pop the top and chug the whole thing. It does nothing for me, though. It doesn't ease the ache or make my heart stop bleeding.

I crush the can with one hand and throw it into the trash on my way out to the couch.

As soon as I lay down, my mind starts playing back all the things I did to Elyse today. Fuck, I hurt her in the worst possible ways. I lied to her, treated her like she meant nothing to me, and then I took her innocence.

But the worst part of all is she still looks at me like she cares. As if I deserve any of her affection, attention, or even her after what I've done.

It would be so much fucking easier if she just hated me. *Why can't she see how bad I am for her?* At the same time, I'm not sure I'll let her go. Yeah, I tried pushing her away, but my heart bleeds for her. The day I kissed her, I knew she was it for me. I fucking knew it.

Sighing, I close my eyes, trying to force myself to go to sleep. Sleep. That's what I need, that'll make me treat her right, right? I almost snort at my thoughts, shifting around on the couch as I try to find a comfortable spot.

As soon as I'm comfortable and my eyes start to drift closed, I hear the bedroom door creak open, and my heart starts racing all over again. It's almost completely dark inside my apartment, but I can still make out her small silhouette against the dim light coming from the window.

I swallow, watching her like a fucking creep.

She walks into the room on tiptoes, and I figure she's going to the kitchen to grab something to drink or maybe eat. Shit, it dawns on me then I didn't even offer her a sandwich or glass of water. I feel like an even bigger asshole—take her virginity, but don't even give her food.

Yeah, I'm a total asshole.

Shock fills my veins when she heads straight for me, her feet making small pitter-patters against the floor. What the hell she is going to do? Stab me? Smother me with a pillow?

Yeah, I wish I could kill myself too.

I remain very still and pretend to be asleep. I don't even think I'd try to stop her if she wanted to punch me in the face. I'm surprised as hell when she starts climbing on top of me, so surprised I forget to tell her no. Bracing herself with both hands on my shoulders, she lowers onto my body.

Then she does something crazy, something that breaks every single fucking rule I've put into place in the last seven days. She rests her beautiful little head against my chest, right above my heart where I know she can hear it beating, and whispers, "I love you." So softly, it's almost inaudible. I want to scream the same words right back at her. I want to tell her how much I love her, how much I want her, but I don't. I can't. Not yet. My only hope right now is she realizes my heart beats only for her—only for *us*.

WHEN I OPEN MY EYES, it takes me a minute to realize where I am. Even my own living room looks unfamiliar when I'm used to waking up in my bed. I stretch and groan. Memories of last night slam into me, each one making me cringe a little bit more than the next.

Elyse.

Where is she?

She was here with me when I fell asleep. I scan the room, but I'm alone. The bedroom door is wide open, but I don't see her in there either.

I start to panic—like a serious fucking panic. If anything happens to her…

My heart races as I run through my apartment searching every room like a lunatic. My feet freeze in front of the closed bathroom door and my ears perk up when I hear the water running.

Sucking fresh air into my lungs, I sigh in relief, waiting for my heart rate to return to a normal speed. *She is here, safe,* I remind myself. I clench my fists. I seriously need to get a grip on my emotions when it comes to her. If I don't, this will all be for nothing…

Opening the bathroom door, I'm hit with a hot cloud of steam.

"What happened last night can't happen again," I announce. I'm not sure why I blurt out these words, but I need her to know, and I can't share with her how much her not being there when I woke up scared me.

Elyse pokes her head out from behind the shower curtain. The color of her hair seems darker. She drips water all over the place, her eyes meeting mine for a brief second. "Well, good morning to you too, and yes, I slept well, thank you for asking." Dipping her head back behind the curtain, she continues, "Breakfast you say? Yes, sure, I'd love to have breakfast with you. Thank you for the kind invite."

I can't miss the giggle of laughter that fills the room. God, she is so fucking adorable, it's sick. "I'm serious. Last night was a lapse in judgement on my part, and it won't happen again.

From here on out, you will sleep in my room, in my bed, alone." I force myself to finish the sentence. Sleeping with her is the only time I get any sleep. She's like a security blanket...like a damn teddy bear, and I don't want to fucking give her up.

She laughs some more and starts humming, clearly ignoring me. With a roll of my eyes, I leave the room, slamming the door shut behind me. I stomp back into the kitchen and open the fridge to evaluate its contents. Shit—not good.

There's half a six pack, a bottle of ketchup, a jar of pickles, and some leftover Chinese food from three days ago. Mmm, breakfast of champions.

I slam the door shut on that too. Grocery shopping it is. I head into my bedroom and get dressed in jeans and a t-shirt. Then I sit down on my bed and wait not so patiently for Elyse to get done in the bathroom.

The minutes tick by ever so fucking slowly.

I fiddle with my fingers. Having her here at my place for whoever knows how long is going to be torture of the worst kind. My room already smells of her—flowers, sunshine, and fucking happiness. It's disgusting, and beautiful. Her things are already spread around here like they belong here, like she lives here. I swallow, my mouth dry. The longer I sit, the more I think, and the more I think...well, the worse it is for me.

Memories of last night keep invading my mind. Like a nightmare on repeat, I'm reminded why I've never loved someone or even considered loving someone other than my mother.

And still, I did something crazy. I'd never fucked a girl without a condom before, but with Elyse, it was different. With her, I didn't want there to be anything between us. I wanted to feel her. Every quiver, every pulse, every flutter of her pussy—I wanted to feel, deep down inside me. Truth be told, pregnancy was the farthest thing from my mind.

All my life, I've been worried about that with other girls,

even more so than getting an STD. Since the moment I first got my dick wet, I've been scared of getting some poor girl pregnant, so I always wrap up, no matter what.

But thinking of Elyse, her belly growing round with our baby, awakens some primal need I wasn't even aware I had. My cock jumps at the thoughts assaulting me. Fuck, I know it's going to be hard to keep my hands off her, and even harder now thinking of all the ways I can make her mine and seal our fates.

The sound of the bathroom door opening fills my ears and I push the thoughts so far down, I hope I won't ever find them again. "Get dressed. We need to go grocery shopping." My voice is deep and doesn't even sound like it belongs to me.

Elyse stops dead in her tracks. Her skin is red from the heat of the water and her hair is wrapped up in a towel that sits perfectly on her head. She looks absolutely stunning. I want to devour her right now—right fucking now.

"I need to go back to my place."

I blink, as if I didn't hear her.

"I could meet you back here later," she continues.

Did she not fucking hear me yesterday? The fact that she is so naive to the bad things in the world is seriously a bad thing. Being as naive as she is could get her killed right now—or worse, raped, or taken into the flesh trades.

I try my best to remain calm when I speak, but there is no easier way to get the words across to her. "Fuck no. You're not leaving my side. What did you not understand about anything I told you last night?" I shake my head and move my neck from side to side, trying to ease the tension. "If you must go back to your place, we can do it together, get groceries, then come back here. But sorry, there is no way I'm letting you out of my sight."

I watch her face go from puzzled to excited and wonder what happened to the girl I saw yesterday. Maybe I broke her? I don't really know. All I know is I don't deserve the girl standing in front of me.

Certain she was going to fight me on the matter, I nearly sigh when she doesn't. She nods her head in agreement, and I watch her as she peels the towel from her body, tossing it to the floor. I continue to stare, sitting on my hands afraid, I may reach out and touch her if I get the chance as she gets dressed.

Why do I torture myself like this?

Elyse doesn't seem bothered by it, though. She doesn't say anything. She just watches me watching her. Like it's a completely fucking normal thing to do.

When we walk out of my apartment and over to my car, I have to fight the urge not to take her hand into my own. Instead, I take out my phone and scroll through my contacts. I find Damon's name on the list and hit the green call button.

I hold the phone up to my ear and listen to it ring, waiting for an answer, but it never comes. His voicemail picks up after the fifth ring. Now, Elyse will be with me until he gets back in touch with me. "Call me back. I need to talk to you," I say after the message tone, trying to keep my voice even so he doesn't get spooked and avoid me on purpose. That'd be a shit mistake on his part. If I don't hear from him soon, I'll just show up at his place, which is the only alternative I have.

I drive over to the dorm first, find a spot close to the door, and park. I kill the engine and pull the keys from the ignition, slipping them into my pocket. When I reach for the door handle, Elyse's voice touches my ears.

"I-I think it'd be better if you don't...come up to my room... with me," she fumbles over her words nervously.

"Why is that?" I eye her, scoffing.

What is she trying to hide?

"Well..." She starts off bashful, her eyes refusing to meet mine. "Tasha is probably there, and honestly, she's not very fond of you." She pauses for a moment. "Actually, she's scared of you. It's probably best if you stay in the car."

And she should be, I think to myself. Having Tasha scared of me serves me well right now. If she's scared, she'll keep her mouth shut, which means I can keep Elyse safe. But if she slips up, something bad is going to happen.

"Fine," I grit out. I don't really want her going up there alone, but I'll deal with it.

Giving me a soft smile, she slips out of the car and walks gracefully into the dorms.

The entire time she's gone, I'm on the verge of getting out of the car and running up to the dorm room to check on her. I don't really give a damn about what Tasha thinks.

I get my phone out to see how long she's been gone. It's been ten minutes. Five more, and I'm going to storm up there.

I watch the minutes tick by, my patience thinning with every second.

Elyse returns exactly four minutes later carrying a large duffel bag, looking like she's heading to a fun sleepover party at a friend's house.

I shake my head and grip the steering wheel hard. She looks so damn happy.

Doesn't she know this isn't going to work out how she wants?

Giving me a wide smile, she gets into the car, throws her bag on the backseat, and buckles herself up. Then she turns to face me, her eyes dazzling. "Where to now?"

"The grocery store." I pull the keys from my pocket and shove them into the ignition. As I put the car into reverse, Elyse's sweet scent fills the small space.

It fucks with my head. It makes me think things, want things...

Putting the car into drive, half of me hopes Damon calls me, and the other half hopes he doesn't. The longer I have Elyse here with me, the longer I want her to stay, and the longer the thought of us as a couple starts to seem okay.

14

lyse

Holding the steaming bag by one corner, I grab the popcorn out of the microwave and pour it into a large bowl. Hero is already sitting on the couch, getting the movie started. His expression looks grim and a bit annoyed, which goes along with the grumpy mood he's had all day. I thought he would lighten up a little bit at least. It was his idea to pick up a movie after all.

"Hero?" Chewing on my lip, I contemplate asking him a question. With the way his mood has been all day, I don't know if I should risk it, but my curiosity to know more about him outweighs the fear of him shutting down. "Can I ask you something?"

"You can ask me anything you want. I'm not sure I'll have an answer for you, though."

"How do you afford living here?" I watch his facial expression carefully, hoping I didn't ask something that might hit a nerve. Luckily, my question has the opposite effect.

His face softens and his eyes turn a little kinder. "My mom. She left me everything she had. She set up a life insurance policy while I was in prison, before she got sick. She always wanted me to go to college. It was one of her last wishes. That's really the only reason I'm here."

"I'm sorry you lost her." I cover my hand with his, meaning nothing more than to comfort him. But even that innocent touch sends a sexually charged current through us.

"Let's just watch the movie." He pulls his hand away from mine, crossing his arms in front of his chest.

The movie starts, colorful images flicker across the screen, but I can't concentrate long enough to understand what it's about. Loud explosions fill my ears, reminding me Hero picked an action movie. No doubt, he chose the least romantic movie he could find and the most boring ever for me.

I nearly groan as a sex scene starts. A few weeks ago, I would have shriveled up and died from embarrassment, especially with a guy sitting next to me.

Thank goodness it's dark in here. If it wasn't, Hero would be able to see my heated cheeks and the warmth creeping down my neck onto my chest. Clenching my thighs together, I shift uncomfortably on the couch. My panties are soaked, and my body's begging me for things I can't give it.

As if Hero can read my mind, he shifts against the armrest to face me. "If I were to reach between your legs right now, would you be wet? I bet you would be." A smug grin appears on his perfectly sculpted lips. There's a hunger in his eyes that excites me as his gaze roams up and down my body, surveying, watching.

"I can see your nipples through your shirt. They're hard and begging to be sucked."

I watch his hand twitch while talking about my nipples,

knowing he wants to touch me. The large bulge forming under his sweatpants is a dead giveaway if I ever saw one. "I want you to touch me," I admit, my voice seductive. Swallowing hard, I wait for him to move or say something, anything.

Instead, he stills for a moment.

I can see him contemplating what to do with me as my mind screams, *please touch me.*

Finally, he puts me out of my misery. He nods his head slightly, signaling for me to move over.

I crawl the short distance, settling into the spot beside him.

"I do have something to make up to you."

His words make it hard to swallow, hard to breathe. When he lifts his hand to my breast and cups it through my shirt, I nearly come unglued.

Even the thin material seems to be way too much of a barrier between us as I consider ripping it off my body and tossing it over my shoulder. "What do you mean?" I don't even know why I'm asking him. *Who cares?* He's touching me, and that's all that matters right now.

He rolls a nipple between his thumb and index finger, coaxing a moan from deep inside me. I find myself leaning into his touch, wanting him, needing him, more and more.

I lift my hand, trailing it across the leather before reaching his quickly stiffening member. Just as my fingers ghost over the cotton of his sweats, he snatches my hand up, his fingers interlocking with mine. "No. This is all about you, baby—all about you." He sighs deeply, as if he's letting all his emotions out, exhaling the exhaustion, the pain, the anger. "Last night...I should have been more..." He pauses, shame filling his green eyes. "I don't know how to explain it, but I should've treated you better. I should've given you more. You deserved better, that's all."

Watching him struggle to find the right words makes my heart beat up into my throat.

Happiness radiates deep inside me, pushing through the broken pieces. Knowing the Hero I fell in love with is still in there gives me hope. I nod, too overwhelmed with emotion to get a word out.

"Stand up," he orders softly.

I eagerly comply. So eager, I make him chuckle with genuine laughter. With agile fingers, he dips into the waistband of my flannel pajamas and starts to pull them down.

His rough knuckles skim down my legs, leaving a burning trail of lava behind. So caught up in his touch and the fire building in my veins, I don't even realize he's pulling down my panties until the cool air hits my wet folds.

"Sit on my lap," he whispers, leaving my clothes in a puddle by my feet.

I step out of them and climb onto his lap, straddling him so I can see his face. My knees rest against the cold leather and a shiver runs through me.

Hero reaches out, placing his hands on my knees. They remain there for a beat, then he starts moving them ever so slowly, dragging them up my thighs.

His thumbs glide along the inside of my thigh where the skin is so sensitive, it makes me giggle. Back and forth. Back and forth. Leaving one hand on my thigh, he moves the other closer and closer to my center.

My breath hitches as he finally reaches the destination. My body tightens. When the rough pad of his thumb touches my already swollen clit, I almost come.

He adds just a little pressure, and my hips start moving on their own. Grinding into him, wanting, needing more. "I need you," I confess, looking into his eyes, hoping to see the same want. I need him to know how much truth is in my words and I'm scared to death to admit how much I need him.

"I know." His voice is low and raw. He moves his hand, keeping his thumb on my clit while probing my entrance with the tip of his middle finger. "Are you sore?" he whispers, his breath fanning against my lips, beckoning me forward.

I think about it for a moment, testing his finger as it slides into me. Rocking my hips forward into his hand a little more, I feel little sparks of pain, but the need for him is too overwhelming, the pleasure he can give me outweighs any pain.

I want him so bad.

All of him—all the time.

"Please?" I whimper.

At my words, I watch his eyes turn a shade darker, then he slips his finger into me all the way.

My back arches, and a loud moan roars from my throat. I grab onto his shoulders, suddenly needing the support. My eyes want to close, but I force them to stay open. I want to see Hero. I want to see him for every moment of this. He keeps thrusting in and out of me while keeping pressure on my clit with his thumb.

I feel like I'm burning up from the inside out. Every fiber in my body is scorching, the flames burning me alive. I'm panting and moaning so loudly, I briefly wonder about the neighbors hearing me.

Hero stares back at me like I'm the only person in the whole world, and I wish nothing more than for him to always look at me this way.

The pressure deep inside me keeps building and building and I come to a point where I can't keep my eyes open any longer. They squeeze shut as the sensations overwhelm my body. Waves of pleasure drown me, consume me, leaving me behind like a jellyfish washed up on the beach.

I lean forward, resting my clammy forehead against Hero's as the last tremors run their course throughout my body. I sink blissfully into his warmth, his entire body encompassing mine. I try to open my eyes again, but the stupid things won't work. I feel comfortable and tired, so damn tired.

Hours, or maybe even minutes tick by, and I'm faintly aware of Hero picking me up and carrying me somewhere.

My head falls into the softness of the pillow, and his manly scent washes over me as he places me on the bed.

He covers me with a blanket, his lips pressing faintly against my forehead. I want to ask him to stay, but I'm too far gone. Half my brain is already asleep, and in the next instant, so is the other half.

Sometime in the middle of the night, I wake up. The room is dark, and it takes me a moment to regain my bearings.

I frown. I'm in Hero's bed, but it feels wrong without him here. The room is empty and cold, and I feel alone, so alone.

Remembering how he carried me to bed last night, I almost kick myself for being too tired to make him stay, or at least try to.

I throw the covers back, uncovering my legs, quickly realizing I'm bare from the belly down. Ugh, he must not have wanted to disturb me. Sneaking out into the living room on tiptoes, I grab my pajamas from the floor and slip them on.

Hero is laying on the couch, his eyes pinched closed, his breathing even.

I can't help but stand there like a stalker and watch him sleep. The only light in the room shines in through the window, and though it's a small sliver, it's enough for me to make out his well-defined chest as it rises and falls in an even rhythm.

I nibble on my bottom lip, quietly shuffling back and forth on my feet. My eyes never leave his sleeping form.

I wonder if I could lie down without him waking up. I know he said it couldn't happen again, this whole sleeping together thing, but I need him. I need his touch, his warmth. Holding my breath, I crawl on top of him as gently and quietly as possible, just as I did the night before.

He stirs slightly, and I freeze, my muscles tensing, the air in my lungs stilling. I hear him mumble something in his sleep, but can't make out what he's saying.

Once I'm sure he's back in a deep sleep, I lay my head down all the way, until my cheek is pressed flat against his chest.

My eyes close at the calming sound of his beating heart. I take a deep, slow breath. The mixture of Hero's shower gel and his own unique scent rushes through my nose, filling in the final missing piece.

This is it. I'm home.

15

Hero

I don't dream often, and when I do, it's mostly nightmares about the night I took my stepfather's life. Not tonight, though. Tonight, I'm dreaming about my sweet Elyse. In my dream, we're happy and worry-free, holding hands, kissing, laughing...

We're *together*.

We are outside, walking on a sunny day. The air is sticky. Her hair shimmers golden in the sunlight, and her skin glows with happiness. I tell a joke, making her giggle, and can't help but pull her into my arms and hold her tightly to my chest. Closing my eyes, I bury my face into the crook of her neck and breathe her essence in. Her flowery smelling hair tickles my nose as I do.

When I open my eyes again, her giggles have vanished, and the sunny outdoor scenery is replaced with the dull backdrop of my living room ceiling.

The only thing that remains the same is Elyse in my arms. Her small, warm body molded to mine, her head using my chest as a pillow. She must have snuck back in here sometime last night. I can't believe I didn't wake up. I should wake her up or carry her back to the bed. This is bad. I've already let this go way too far. I need to make her understand we need to keep a distance between us.

Glancing down at her half-covered face, looking like an angel, I can't bring myself to wake her up. I watch her sleep for almost an hour...and could have watched a few hours more.

Her breathing changes, and she stirs on top of me, stretching her sleepy limbs and rubbing her leg against my already stiff dick.

"I really need you to get off me..." *Before I bend you over the couch and fuck you senseless.*

"What's wrong?" she asks in a sleepy voice.

Is she trying to play fucking innocent with me, like she doesn't really know what she's doing? I push her up with me so we can both sit instead of laying on top of one another. "You can't keep doing this, okay?" I try to keep my voice calm, not wanting to yell at her first thing in the morning. Hell, if I had it my way, I'd never yell at her, but she keeps pushing me, testing my damn boundaries.

"Why can't we sleep together in the bed?" she deadpans, as if I hadn't already told her why.

"I already explained this to you. I told you what this was from the very beginning. Only sex, no cuddling after, no emotional shit. Nothing." Now, I'm pissed. Why is she making this so hard? Why can't she just listen to me? I want to throttle her, shake her until it all makes sense to her.

Before I can, she shakes her head at me, dismissing my words as if she never heard them. "Stop! Stop pretending like there's nothing between us and this doesn't mean anything to you." She gestures to the space between us. "Stop pretending I don't mean anything to you." Defeat coats her words.

"You don't..." Saying the words hurts so fucking much, but I force them out anyway and continue digging my own grave. "You mean nothing to me, Elyse. *Nothing.* How many times do I need to tell you this before you get it into your head? Or are you just too fucking stupid to understand?"

The air between us sizzles. I know I've made a mistake the moment I see her tiny hand headed toward my face. I don't even have a chance to brace for the slap.

The flat of her palm connects with my cheek and the sound of skin slapping skin resonates through the room. My cheek burns and stings upon impact.

Her slap may have hurt, but nothing hurts more than the look in her eyes.

Fury and sadness reflect back at me as the next words fall from her lips. "You think this is what your mom would have wanted for you? You pretending to be an asshole so you can hide your real feelings? You think she would've wanted this life for you? To treat me this way?" The tears swim in her eyes, but she's strong, stronger than I've ever seen her.

Well, she's going to need to be stronger if she wants to win this. "My mother is dead, so I don't think often about what she would think of me, and even if she were alive, it's not like it would matter. I killed a man in cold blood, Elyse. I literally beat the shit out of him with my bare hands and strangled him until he stopped breathing. I highly doubt she would bat an eyelash at the way I'm treating you now." My voice is neutral even though I'm dying on the inside, one single sliver away from breaking down and apologizing.

Elyse doesn't deserve this treatment, not after growing up the way she did. She needs love, affection, a man worthy of her time, and I am not him. The little shit show with Damon proved that much.

I'm going one way, and she's going another.

"Well..." she hiccups, and I pray to god she doesn't start crying. I'm already clenching my fists so tight, the muscles ache. The last thing I need is to fucking lash out and break something, and that will happen if she starts crying.

"I think your mom would expect more from you, and I think if she were here, she'd want you to be happy. You protected her, you were her hero, and now..." She pauses briefly, her chest heaving. "Now, you're mine. Even if you don't want to be, you're mine."

I can't do this with her—I can't. Shoving from the couch, I stride across the room with purpose, my fist begging for something to hit. I walk into the kitchen and lean against the counter, my thoughts swirling...all of them about Elyse.

Do I push her away?

Do I pull her in?

I slam my closed fist on the counter. My body shakes, my nails biting into my palm as I try to get a grip on reality. The sound of my cell phone ringing off in the distance pulls me from my manic thoughts.

I rush into my bedroom and pluck the device up off the dresser, pressing the answer key as soon as I see Damon's name scroll across the screen.

"Hey. What's up?" he chimes, his voice casual, cool, calm.

"Hey. You get my message?" I try to hide the anger in my voice.

"Yeah. What's up?" He's acting all nonchalant, and it's only fucking with my temper more.

"I'm going to meet you at the warehouse tonight. I don't want to talk about it over the phone," I lie. When I ask Damon about Elyse, I need to look him in the eyes.

"Warehouse? Let's meet at Night Shift instead. I've got business to attend to there, so it will make it easier for both of us." I don't know how Elyse will feel about going to a strip club, but she's just going to have to suck it up. If this is the only place Damon is willing to meet, so be it.

"Cool. See you there at ten." I hang up the phone and turn to Elyse, curiously eyeing me from across the room. "Ever been to a strip club?" I ask, like I don't already know the answer.

16

lyse

"*Ever been to a strip club?*" Hero's voice mocks in my head all day long. He's cranky and irritable while he does everything he can to avoid me, which is pretty damn hard when we're in the same house. I try to forget about my confession, forget about the feelings spiraling out of control inside me.

I force myself to remain in Hero's bedroom most of the day, my books and homework sprawled out on his bed. I immerse myself in my studies so I don't start crying—or worse, get into another argument with him.

I'm working on putting study guide cards together when Hero appears in the doorway with a paper plate in his hand.

He looks mouthwatering. His midnight black hair is disheveled, his eyes are a soft green instead of their usual dark green, and he's wearing jeans and a t-shirt—a t-shirt that clings to his perfectly sculpted body.

"Hungry?" he asks gruffly.

I don't say anything, even though my stomach has been grumbling for the last two hours. "Sure." I shrug.

He walks into the bedroom, coming to a stop at the foot of the bed, his eyes moving over all the books and papers sitting on it. He pauses for a long time before extending the paper plate out to me.

I eye the contents of the plate curiously. A sandwich and a bag of chips.

"Sorry. I'm not much of a cook, and we don't have a lot of time. A sandwich it is."

I don't complain, food is food. Plus, Hero made it. "It's fine. Thank you." I give him a sad smile and redirect my attention to my books. Having him this close makes my heart beat faster, saliva in my mouth pool, and ignites the fire in my belly.

He's got a hold on me, and it consumes my every thought. The idea that this might be my last night here saddens me more than I care to let on. He's pushing me away, weaseling distance between us slowly, and I miss him so much, it kills me.

I pick at the sandwich, my appetite evaporating into thin air. I want to cry. I want to slap him and knock the sense back into him. But it doesn't matter. It won't work. I think about my options, about the things my parents want from me, about what I want.

Hero interrupts my thoughts by pulling his phone out of his pocket. He looks at the screen for half a second, then shoves it back into his pocket, his eyes lifting to mine. "Hate to cut your eating short, but we've got to get going."

I nod, swallowing the small bite of food still in my mouth. I stack my books up and close my notebook before moving off the bed. Then I look down at my clothes. "Is this okay to wear?" I ask.

Hero's gaze sweeps over me. It's possessive, hungry, and I'd bet anything if I touched him right now, he'd melt beneath my touch.

"It's fine. We're going for business, Elyse, not pleasure. Unless you'd like me to leave you there and you can work something out with Damon on your own."

I blink, not sure what Damon has to do with all this. He says talking to Damon will help determine if someone is watching me, but I don't understand how. Is he with the FBI? A private agent? Why is this guy so special? Then, it hits me. I never once figured out who that guy Hero was helping was...or the guy slumped over in the chair.

The questions linger on my tongue.

"I don't even want to go, let alone be left there."

"Well, you are, so get your fucking shoes on and head toward the door."

Half of me wants to fight him while the other half just wants to comply. I know what's going to happen after all this is done, and I'm dreading it.

As if Hero can read my mind, he takes a warning step toward me. Am I supposed to be afraid of him? "Don't make this harder than it needs to be. Just do what I tell you to. Keep your mouth fucking shut and nothing bad will happen."

I cross my arms over my chest, staring him down, refusing to let him treat me like dirt. "And what if I don't, then what happens?"

He remains very still. The air between us sizzles. It's so hot, I can feel it zinging against my skin.

Hero is tense, angry, and...it turns me on.

"Death. Rape. I don't fucking know, Elyse. But there is more to this than you and me. If you want to make it out of his alive, you'll listen to me..."

I gulp around the bubble of fear forming in my throat.

Death? Rape? How deep does this go? What has Hero gotten himself into? I knew he was dark and had a past, that he was hiding things, but now, I'm reconsidering everything. He keeps pushing me, farther and farther away, claiming it's what's best for me, and for so long, I've told him it isn't.

But maybe he's right—maybe he's been right all along.

WE PULL into the parking lot of Night Shift. I only know this because of the half-lit neon sign that hangs on the front of the building. The place makes bile rise into my throat and my stomach churn. I think I might puke. I fidget with my hands as Hero kills the engine. I've never been to such a vulgar place.

He shifts in his seat to face me. It's so dark outside, it makes it hard to see him.

"I can see your nervousness from a mile away, and they will too. Stop fidgeting, take some deep breaths, and calm down."

I do as he says, but the air refuses to enter my lungs. It feels like everything is tightening, disallowing to let even a single molecule of air in. "Do I have to go in? I can just stay out here and wait for you." My voice is filled with worry, my thoughts consumed with the fact that this might be the last time I'm alive. Why would Hero bring me here? Why would he subject me to this?

To make an example. The thought appears inside my head before I can stop it.

Hero shakes his head at my question. "No. You're going inside with me. I can't trust you'll be safe in here, especially not where we are right now."

My hands shake as I reach for the door handle. I want to glue myself to the seat. But if I don't get out and go inside, Hero will force me, and that'll be one hundred times worse.

Digging deep inside myself, past the fear and sadness, I open the car door and step out onto the pavement. There's a cold breeze, and I realize I should've brought a jacket. Hero walks in front of me instead of beside me, his strides full of purpose and strength. He's walking with his head held high, while I'm shivering in fear.

As we get closer to the building, I see a guy standing outside it. His face doesn't hold an ounce of emotion, and he doesn't even look at Hero and I as we slide inside. I wrinkle my nose at the smells assaulting my nose.

Smoke clings to the air, and I start to cough as I suck the tainted air into my lungs.

Hero pulls me into his side as we travel deeper into the building. There's a dimly lit bar off to the right side of the room, and a huge stage where lights flash in several colors. I know what a strip club is. I might be naive and sheltered, but I'm not stupid.

Music softly plays in the background, and I notice quite a few men lingering at tables near the stage. Hero doesn't pay any attention to these things, though. He just keeps walking, almost as if he's angry. We veer off to the left, down a long, dark hall, then take another left.

I can hear someone moaning off in the distance and look up at Hero to ask him about it. He merely shakes his head at me. My mind starts to wander. The woman sounds like she's happy, but is she really? Are they abusing her? Hurting her?

We stop a moment later in front of a door. It's painted red, and I wonder if that's because they bring people into this room to kill them.

A large, burly man with fists of steel and menacing eyes stares me down.

I partially hide behind Hero, wanting to run right the hell out of this place.

"Who's the girl?" The unknown man gestures to me curiously.

I see the muscle in Hero's jaw jump. Is he jealous? Angry? There's something there...something for me.

"No worries, Diego. She's with me."

Diego pauses, his gaze running up and down my body once more before he raps his knuckles against the wood doorframe.

A second later, a deep voice vibrates through me. "Send him in."

Him? I blink. What does that mean? I don't even get a chance to ask Hero what he's talking about because the door opens and I'm ushered inside, pushed forward by the weight of Hero's body, his fingers digging painfully into my arms. When my eyes land on the man in front of me, the man sitting behind a huge desk, a cigarette hanging from his lips, I know I'm in trouble.

I don't even need to feel it in my bones, not when he pushes from the desk with a gun pointed right at me.

"Damon," Hero grits out.

My heart flutters.

This is Damon. The man from the warehouse finally has a name, and he looks like he's ready to kill me.

17

ero

There are very few moments in my life where I've been afraid, actually afraid, and this—this is one of them. Elyse trembles in my grasp, her tiny body rattling against mine, making me want to protect her. But I can't. I couldn't even if I tried.

"Hero." Damon's voice is slightly unhinged. He looks pissed, irate even. "I thought I told you to get rid of her or I would. This doesn't look like she's been gotten rid of, does it?"

I clench my jaw so tightly, I'm afraid I'm going to break a fucking tooth. If it weren't for Damon being a close friend of mine, a friend who helped me and my mother when I was on the inside, I'd knock the fucker out cold. But because of all he's done, I'm loyal to him to a fault. *But am I loyal enough to give Elyse to him?*

"I'm aware of what you asked of me, and I know for a fact you fucking heard me when I said I wasn't going to get rid of her."

"She's a liability, Hero. Look at her…" Damon snarls, moving from behind the desk.

Elyse shudders against my chest, her face pressing against my body.

"She's shaking like a fucking leaf, and why? Because I'm holding a gun?" The laughter that erupts from him is humorless. "She's literally on the verge of spilling the beans. If she was asked about us, what do you think she'd say?"

I hold Elyse to my chest, feeling every tremble of her body.

She's afraid, scared fucking shitless, but even I know she's loyal to me and would never call the cops or do something to compromise me. "I didn't come here so you could parent me. I came here because I want to know who you have on her." My eyes pierce his, and I swear to god if he lies to me, I'm going to turn his own gun against him. Friend or not. Loyal or not. A liar is a fucking liar.

"Have on her?" Damon takes a drag of his cigarette, his eyes darkening. "She's not worth the trouble. You fucking told me you'd take care of her, so I didn't put anyone on her. It's a waste of my time to get involved, but that doesn't mean I want to lose my best man or compromise my business."

I nod, a different kind of fear and anger taking root inside me. If it's not Damon, then it's someone else—and that terrifies me. If Elyse is being followed, that confirms she needs me.

"But since we have her here, why don't we just get it done with?" Damon takes a step forward, the gun pointed directly at Elyse.

She shifts in my arms to face forward. I can no longer see her face, but I can imagine the terror in her eyes.

"I told you no. I have other ways of dealing with this." I swallow hard.

Damon doesn't seem to care about my response. His eyes remain trained on Elyse. "Do you even know him? Know he did seven years for murder...murder in cold blood, strangling the fuck out of the bastard."

Elyse nods her head.

I feel shame coating me from the inside out. I should've just left her at the fucking house. Then again, look at how far that got me before.

"Do you know how many women he's fucked? Not some pussy ass making love bullshit, but fucked, hard, screaming as they fall apart on his cock. Do you know how many?"

I cringe. When Damon takes another step toward her, the gun still pointed directly at her, his finger on the trigger, I know I have to do something. If Damon shoots me, so be it. I can't let anything happen to Elyse—not when I'm trying to protect her, not when the entire reason I pushed her away was so she wouldn't have to see this.

"I don't care how many women he's been with, and I don't care that he killed someone. He didn't do it because he wanted to." Elyse's sweet voice sounds like it doesn't belong here in this room, or even this world.

"It's so adorable how you think you know him," Damon taunts.

I need to figure out how to diffuse the situation before it gets worse.

"I bet you think he'll stay with you, protect you, cherish you. But that's not Hero. He's not really living up to his name, baby. He's a criminal. Blood covers his hands the same way it does mine. You've seen that part of him, though, so you know. It's living inside him, the dark part, the part that feeds on the innocent."

Elyse shakes her head in disbelief. "Hero lives up to his name every single day. I don't care about what I saw that night, I care about him and the person he is when he's with me."

Tension fills my muscles.

I make a move to put Elyse behind me, but I'm not fast enough. Damon reaches out for her, his fingers sinking into her golden-brown hair. Her neck twists as he drags her from my grasp, forcing her eyes to meet his. He brings the barrel of the gun to her lips, and my entire world sinks away.

"Do you care about him enough to take a bullet for him? To fucking die for him?" Damon acts as if I'm not standing right here.

I clench my fists and unclench them, every possible scenario running rampant inside my mind.

What if he accidentally pulls the trigger?

My heart beats for the person in front of me, for Elyse. If he kills her, if he harms her, I'll kill him and everyone else in this fucking building.

"Let her go, Damon," I order, not wanting to make too much of a scene. There is no hiding Elyse from this life anymore. There's no point in me denying us what we want. Not after this moment.

A sinister smile pulls on Damon's lips as his grip tightens into her hair.

A whimper escapes Elyse's lips, and I move without thinking, letting instinct take over and direct my body.

With the element of surprise, I push the gun in Damon's hand upward with my right and punch him in the ribs with my left. The gun goes off in his hand, a bullet hitting somewhere in the ceiling above us. Damon releases Elyse, and I push her out of the way with my elbow.

She staggers to the side before landing on the hard ground. For a split second, I want to grab her and hold her to my chest and tell her everything will be okay, but I don't know if it will be, and I can't do shit for her while Damon is still a threat in front of me.

His face is contorted with anger and betrayal. He snarls at

me like a wild animal. "You're going to fucking regret coming here." He's still holding his gun, finger on the trigger.

If I let his hand down, he will shoot us. He swings for me with his free hand, hitting my jaw. My head snaps to the side, but I don't feel pain.

All I can think of is Elyse and how she's in danger because of me. I'm going to get her hurt...all over again.

How many times am I going to fuck up?

"Hero..." Hearing her say my name like a prayer is all I need to find that extra strength to twist Damon's hand, making him drop the gun to the floor.

He reaches for it, but I'm faster. I lift the gun, pointing it in his direction, something I would have never thought I'd be doing.

Damon takes a small step back, putting his hand up, showing me his palms. He shakes his head at me tightly, as if he can't believe I'm holding a gun on him.

"I can't let you hurt her." I look into his eyes so he knows I mean every word I say. "I love her, and I will not let anybody hurt her. Not even you."

At my admission, his face changes.

I lower the gun to point it toward the ground between us. I don't want to hurt him, but I will. I know I will. "We have been through a lot together, Damon. You are the closest thing I have to a friend. Don't ruin it over this."

"Don't get all sappy on me now," he huffs. "Fine, I'll leave her alone. But I'm warning you, if I hear of her yapping about me to anyone, she is done."

Hearing him threatening her doesn't put me at ease, but this is the best I'm going to get out of Damon right now. I change the grip on the gun to hand it over to him before I crouch down to Elyse and pick her up from the ground. I slip my arm around her waist and pull her close to my side.

She hasn't stopped shaking, and I doubt she will until we are out of here. I'll make this up to her tenfold, but right now, she's going to have deal with it. She leans into me, and I pull her even closer.

"I still need to figure out who's watching Elyse. If it's not you, then it's someone else. I could use your help with that. I'll pay you, of course." Friend or not, Damon doesn't do anything for free. You either work for him or you pay him. One way or another, I'm at his mercy.

He puts his gun back into his holster and takes a seat in the large leather chair behind his desk. His fingers drum against his chin, his eyes narrowing in thought. "I don't need any more money right now. What I need is some extra muscle around here. I'm down a guy, and it just so happens you would be perfect for that job."

"I don't want to be involved in any more of this, Damon."

"That's the deal. Take it or leave it," he smirks, knowing damn well I'm going to take it.

My eyes skirt down to Elyse. Her body's still trembling slightly, her blue eyes sad. I don't want to agree to anymore shit that could potentially endanger her or what we have, but I have to protect her. "Fine," I sigh. "I'm not starting tonight, though. I'm taking her home. Call me tomorrow with details."

"Glad we got that settled. Go home and tuck your girl in... unless you want to get one of the other girls and have a threesome with her."

The way he looks at Elyse is sickening. I want to punch him in the face all over again.

Saving it for another day, I usher Elyse out the door, never losing my hold on her. I open the car door for her, and make her sit down, then I buckle her in. She seems to be in shock, unable to say anything, and I'm okay with that. I'll give her time to breathe...time to come to terms with it all.

I drive straight home, wanting her somewhere she feels the most safe and comfortable. I cut off the engine and get out of the car, but Elyse doesn't make a move. I open her door and gently get her out. "Come on, baby. I've got you."

She grabs onto my shoulder and lets me help her. "You said you love me." She tilts her head up to look into my eyes.

"I did. Let's get you inside, then we'll talk about everything."

The moment we enter my apartment, I feel a million times better. My mind flickers through the events that took place. Until now, it hadn't really sunk in that I could have lost Elyse today.

She might be the one in shock, but I am a fucking mess.

I help her out of her sweater, catching a whiff of smoke and booze. It clings to our clothes, reminding me further how close Elyse was to death because of me.

"Why don't we take a shower before we go to bed?" I suggest, knowing it's most likely what she needs.

"Okay." Her voice is still a little shaky, but already sounds so much stronger than it did a few minutes ago.

We walk into the bathroom, and I start undressing her, leaving all her clothes in a pile next to the tub. I hate how quiet she is. The permanent frown on her lips, it breaks my fucking heart.

Turning on the water, I check the temperature before I let her get in. I strip out of my own clothes, adding them to the pile, and get into the shower behind her.

As soon as I step in, she leans her back against my front, and I wrap my arms around her stomach. She lets her head fall back to rest on my shoulder like she needs this...like she needs me.

Lowering my head, I kiss her neck, and a sensual moan escapes her plump lips. My dick twitches in excitement at the sound, and I pull back an inch. She doesn't need this right now.

She's in shock, afraid. I grab the soap and squirt some into my palm. I start washing her shoulders, massaging them, kneading all the tension from her body.

"That feels so good." She turns in my arms, and I start massaging her front, giving extra attention to her breasts. My thumb skims across her hardened nipple, and I listen as an audible gasp fills her lungs. I do it again, to the same nipple, and am rewarded with the same breathless tone.

Her beautiful blue eyes flutter closed, and she teeters on her feet before leaning into me more.

"Hero," she whimpers against my skin, her lips blazing a trail of fire over my chest.

Fuck, I wanted this to be more than this, but my dick is hard as steel.

I take down the showerhead to rinse us both off quickly. I don't want to fuck her in the shower. I want her in my bed. I want to cherish and worship her body like I should have done the first time.

Using the fluffiest towel I have, I dry her off from top to bottom before I dry off myself and lead her to my—*our* bed.

"Lie down, baby..." I watch her as she crawls into my bed and lies with her head on my pillow.

Her still wet hair falls around her, encompassing her in a halo of golden brown. Her perfect body is spread out in front of me like a feast. Fuck, I can't believe how lucky I am that this beautiful creature is here with me.

Even after all the shit I've put her through, she remains here with me.

Looking up at me with nothing besides love and trust, she says quietly, "I love you."

"I love you too." I climb over the top of her, pressing her small body into the mattress, bringing our bodies as close as possible. We're skin on skin. I can feel her heart pounding against my own.

The need to kiss her consumes me. I dip my head and press my lips against hers. Her fingers run through my hair, her tiny nails indent into my skin, and I relish the feelings spiraling out of control inside me.

Every inch of her I see I want to touch and devour. I want to make every part of her mine.

My mouth moves all over her creamy skin, my tongue dipping in and out, leaving a trail of fire behind. Her moans become louder, her quivers become stronger, and when she arches her back, pushing her pretty pussy against my swollen cock, I know she needs more.

"Please...Hero..." she begs and pleads, as if I wouldn't give her exactly what she wants or needs.

I move up her body and take her lips next, delving my tongue into her hot mouth like I want to drive my dick into her tight pussy.

Nudging her legs apart with my knees, I barely touch her, and she spreads herself wider, making me smile mid-kiss.

Sliding one hand between us, I guide my dick inside her. I go slow at first, letting her adjust to my size. Her tight, hot walls grab onto me, squeezing me so tightly, black colors my vision. It feels so fucking good. I never want to stop fucking her. My dick wants to live inside her permanently.

Her legs wrap around me, pulling me closer to her, deeper. Unable to hold back any longer, I dive into her all the way, until I feel the back of her pussy, then pull out just a little before plunging back in.

She moans directly in my ear, and her small fingers grip onto my arms.

"Does that feel good for you, baby?"

"Yes," she moans, wrapping her legs around me, her heels digging into my butt cheeks.

I find a rhythm, rocking into her, and she tries to match me thrust for thrust, which makes me chuckle. Such a tiny thing trying to own me, own her pleasure. It turns me on more.

With little effort, I lift her pelvis so I hit that spot deep inside her, that magic spot that draws the loudest moans out of her.

It doesn't take her long to come apart. I watch her face closely as she does. Her nose wrinkles, and her mouth parts slightly while her body shimmers and shakes.

She is so fucking beautiful, it hurts. Seeing her like this is the icing on the cake. I want to see her like this every day, and I will if I can help it.

After coming so close to losing her today, I find I need to make one thing clear, with myself, with us. "I'm done wasting time, pushing you away and pretending we are not meant for each other. We might have grown up in different worlds, but we found our way to each other and that's all that matters," I grit out, my jaw tight, my body shaking.

Elyse arches her hips upward, her walls still pulsating around me from her own orgasm when mine finally slams into me.

Blackness overtakes my vision, and I squeeze Elyse to my chest, afraid she may disappear if I don't.

Fuck, I've never come so hard in my life. My balls draw together and my whole body spasms as I empty myself into the depth of her pussy. I slump on top of her, completely spent, putting almost all my body weight on her, but she doesn't seem to mind.

Her soft fingers trace the tattoos on my arms. I don't want to move, and I definitely don't want to pull out of her.

"We didn't use a condom," she whispers, sounding neither nervous nor angry.

"I know." I probably should have asked her if this was okay first, but I just don't want there to be anything between us. Not even a thin layer of latex. If she gets pregnant, I'll take care of her...and our baby.

After a few minutes, I find the strength to roll over, taking Elyse with me so she's laying on top of me instead of the other way around.

"Goodnight, baby," I whisper into her hair before I fall into the deepest sleep I've ever experienced.

18

lyse

My phone ringing drags me out of the most amazing sleep of my life. My limbs are entangled with Hero's, and he's breathing heavily into my hair, his breath tickling my neck.

It takes me a while to get free from the weight of his heavy arm slung across my body. By some miracle, I get free without waking him up.

I grab my phone from the floor and check who's calling me so early. Could be Tasha, though I doubt it. My mom maybe? My eyes glance over the screen. It is, in fact, my mother.

Sneaking out of the room, I don't answer the phone until I'm in the living room. The last thing I want to do is wake Hero up.

"Hello?" I try to keep my voice down.

"Elyse, it's your mother."

I roll my eyes. *I know who you are, and even if I didn't, my caller ID would tell me.*

"I'm at your dorm. I was hoping we could grab some breakfast."

"Oh, I'm at...a friend's house." I hate lying, but technically, I'm not. You can be in love with someone and that person could still be your friend, right?

"Why don't you meet me at that coffee place on the corner?" my mom says without missing a beat. But something about what she says doesn't seem right.

Normally, she would have questioned my whereabouts by now. Has she finally realized I'm not a child anymore? I doubt that. All of this seems strange, even for her. "The Starbucks? Yes, sure, I can meet you there in, say, twenty minutes?" Maybe even thirty. I smile to myself. That's what she gets for showing up unannounced...*again*.

"Perfect. I'll see you then." She hangs up, and I shake my head. She's acting weird, and the fact that she's here to see me without my father is even stranger.

I sneak back into the bedroom to check on Hero. Cracking the door, I peer inside. Thankfully, he's still sleeping peacefully, just like a baby. As I stare at him, I debate whether I should let him sleep or wake him up.

The blanket is only covering him up to his belly button. His muscular chest, broad shoulders, and well-defined arms are exposed and on display. I wipe at my mouth as if I'm drooling.

Holy hell, I never knew a man could be so gorgeous.

My eyes make their way up to his face, relaxed in his sleep. With his constant frown gone, he appears years younger. It's a look I could get used to seeing on his face.

Watching him sleeping so peacefully, I decide to let him be. I know he might be angry to discover I left without letting him know or waking him, but that's a risk I'm willing to take. I do not want my mother to see him and put him down some more. I'd rather skip that scene altogether. And honestly, I shouldn't really be gone that long. I continue to contemplate my options.

I don't want to make Hero angry, not after everything last night.

I nibble on my bottom lip. Maybe I could just go see my mom really quick, pick up coffee for us both, and be back before he even wakes up? And even if he wakes up before I get back, surely he wouldn't be mad at me for getting coffee, right?

I softly sigh. I know what I have to do...

Grabbing my bag, I make my way into the bathroom and make myself presentable for the outside world. When I'm done, I peek into the bedroom one last time. I smile to myself as I eyeball him once more.

Nope, hasn't moved an inch.

I'm nearly out the door when I have the bright idea to leave a note. Signing with a heart under my name, I scribble a note on a piece of paper I found on the counter telling Hero where I'm going. I leave it on the kitchen table where he can see it right away and head out to see my mom. I walk briskly and make it there in just under twenty minutes from the time she called, but that doesn't stop my mother from scowling at me like I'm an hour late.

When I sit down across from her at one of the small tables, I notice her looking past my shoulder. It seems like she's expecting someone else to show up.

Curious, I too turn my head, scanning the crowd. No familiar faces or abnormal people catch my eye, so I turn back around. Clearly, my mother's paranoia is getting the best of her.

"So, Elyse, I came here to talk to you about something."

I blink, annoyance slamming into me. She talks to me like I'm dumb and incapable of my own thinking. As if I didn't know she came here to talk to me about something. Most parents come to visit their kids because they miss them. My mother comes to tell me something.

"Something you couldn't tell me over the phone?" I question, my brow raised.

"Elyse..." She leans forward and reaches across the table like she is about to take my hand in hers.

Nope, not doing that. Pulling my hand away before her fingers can even graze mine, I straighten myself.

My mom clears her throat, looking slightly hurt. She then pulls her hand back and places it in her lap before continuing. "Elyse, I really think you need to take a good look at yourself and reflect on what you are doing here. People at church have been talking about you, about *us*. Who do you think is going to marry you if you are *impure*?" she mumbles over the word as if just saying it out loud will make her a bad person.

With her insults hanging in the air, I stare into her unapologetic eyes, my mouth hanging wide open. "Mom, first of all, it's none of your business what I'm doing before marriage. Second, I don't care what the people at church think about me...or you, for that matter. Also, please stop showing up unannounced just to try guilting me into coming home." By now, I'm seething with rage. Had I known this would be a guilt fest, I'd have just stayed in bed with Hero.

"I'm not trying to make you feel bad, I just want you to come home and be with your family...where you belong. Your siblings miss you too, you know. Come home before it's too late." My mom is clearly struggling to keep her voice calm after my little outburst.

Unfortunately, for both of us, I have already reached the end of my rope.

"I belong here...with Hero. I am not coming home, and since you are so concerned with my virginity and being *pure*, I'll have you know I've lost that already."

Apparently, that wasn't the right thing to say. My mother sucks in a sharp breath and her face goes crimson. She jumps up from her seat, just to slam her hands down on the table with a loud smack, alerting everyone in the building.

All eyes are on us as my mom leans toward me, and yells,

"You should be ashamed of yourself, being a disgrace to our family. I can't believe I've raised such a whore."

My whole body freezes. I can't even blink, but it only takes me about five seconds to compose myself and decide this is the last straw for me. I can't keep subjecting myself to this behavior. I left for college for a reason. I was lucky I got out and don't have to deal with this—them. Not anymore.

"I don't want to see you here ever again." Surprised at how I even manage my voice to come out, I get up and march out the door.

Without thinking about it, I use my hand with the hurt wrist to push the door open. A sharp pain radiates through my arm, reminding me of my mistake.

I grit my teeth and keep walking. Right now, I welcome that pain. I'd rather concentrate on that than thinking about what my mom just said to me.

Rage simmers deep inside me. She didn't even ask about my wrist, or acknowledge it, for that matter. What kind of mother does that?

She had to have seen it, but clearly, her concern for my wellbeing is not the most important thing. All she's worried about is what people might think about her...about my family, about my purity.

Walking back to Hero's place takes me half the time since I'm basically speed walking. I should have never answered that call. I could have stayed in bed with Hero, instead of allowing my mom to tell me what a horrible person I am.

It isn't until I'm in front of Hero's door I realize I don't have a key to his place. God, this is just getting worse by the second. Lifting my hand to the bell, I'm just about to press it when the door swings open.

A now fully dressed Hero rushes out so quickly, he almost knocks me over.

I blink while steadying myself.

"Elyse, what the fuck?"

Before I have a chance to respond, or do a thing, his arms engulf me in a bear hug, pulling me to his chest so tightly, I can hardly breathe. The air in my lungs stills, and I wonder if he's just happy to see me.

He lets go of me, just enough to be able to pull me into the house and shut the door behind us. "Why didn't you wake me up? I told you not to go anywhere by yourself."

Caught off guard by his angry tone, I try to take a step back, but there's nowhere to go. Hero still has one hand on my forearm, his fingers wrapped around my wrist like an iron shackle that won't budge. "I'm sorry. I thought I would be back before you woke up," I pout.

"Is that supposed to make it better? Do you not understand what it would do to me if something happened to you? Don't you understand what you mean to me?" His eyes are frantic, his face full of worry.

At first glance, Hero seems nothing besides furious. But underneath that anger, I can feel the longing, love, and desperation. Without even thinking, I do the only thing I can in this moment...

I kiss him.

Our lips clash together furiously as the beginning of an all-consuming passionate kiss.

I moan into his mouth while my fingers find their way into his thick black hair. My body arches into his touch as his warmth welcomes me.

His hands are already roaming my body, caressing my backside, tugging and pulling, gripping and holding. Suddenly, he breaks the kiss, but he doesn't pull away fully. Instead, he picks me up and carries me to the edge of the couch.

Still breathless from the kiss, I try to figure out what he's doing.

As soon as my feet hit the floor, his hands roughly pull my

jeans and panties down to my knees. He doesn't even bother to let me step out of them before he turns me to face the couch and bends me over it.

"Hero..." I try to get up, but his hand is between my shoulder blades, pushing my face down into the couch. Panic creeps in on me like a summer rainstorm and I seriously think about screaming. I have to remind myself this is Hero behind me. Even though he's mad at me right now, he would never actually hurt me.

Putting all my trust in him, I stay still and listen as he unbuckles and unzips his pants. The smooth tip of his dick nudges against my entrance. As he leans into me, I feel his hot breath at my ear. "Is this what you want? Are you trying to make me mad? Do you want me to remind you who you belong to?"

"I-I didn't..." At first, I just can't find the right words, then he slams into me, burying himself so deeply, I lose the ability to speak.

He doesn't stop or slow down to wait for me to adjust to his length. His hands grip my hips firmly, holding me in place.

I cry out in a mixture of pleasure and pain, my hands grasping the couch for dear life. I let him take me the way he wants, knowing full well if I ask him to stop, he will. But I don't want him to stop.

The surprise and pain quickly disappear into thin air, leaving me with nothing besides intense pleasure. His cock slams into me savagely, his fingers hold onto me with a bruising grip. I feel satisfied, cared for, possessed. There's something so raw about this, it awakens a primal side of me.

And just like that, I come fast and hard.

Hero doesn't slow, though. He thrusts his hips harder, faster, pumping into me through my orgasm, intensifying it to the point where my vision blurs. I don't know how long he keeps this up. Time seems to stand still. After a while, I can feel myself being pushed to yet another peak. The pleasure is insane as my body shakes at the roughness of his touch.

"You going to come for me again?" Hero leans over, pressing his sweat covered body onto mine, and reaches around me. His fingers find my clit, making me scream out his name. I can feel every single muscle in his body tense. He's dragging this out, enjoying every single stroke inside me.

"That's it...milk my cock, baby."

His crude words combined with his dick buried so deep inside me while his fingers play rigorously against my clit send me into a frenzy. I thought the last orgasm he gave me was intense, but this is out of this world. I can feel every fiber in my body all at once, all joined in one mind-blowing euphoria. Air, my heart beating, none of those things matter.

I never want this feeling to end.

I want to stay in this place of bliss and happiness forever.

I'm faintly aware of Hero grunting and groaning behind me as he pounds into me one last time before stiffening, his hot cum fills me to the brim. He pulses inside me for a short time before relaxing on top of me.

He gets off me a few minutes later, when my heart has finally slowed to a normal beat. I don't understand how he's able to make his body work after what we just did. My limbs feel like cooked spaghetti. There's no way I'll be able to get up any time soon.

I hear Hero leave the room, then water running in the distance.

Is he taking a shower?

Footsteps approach a moment later, and two strong arms slide underneath me to pull me up. I'm back on my feet, looking up at Hero as he gazes down at me, his expression full of concern, and maybe a little guilt. "Are you okay?" His lips ghost against my forehead.

His warm body encompasses me. I want to snuggle into his

chest and never leave. "Yes, just a little weak in the knees." Even my voice sounds drained. I feel like I could sleep another twelve hours if he'd let me.

"Okay. Let's get you into the bath."

That sounds like a great idea. My thighs rub together, and I feel Hero's release sticky against my skin. "I don't think I can walk right now."

At my admission, Hero just picks me up like I'm a small child and carries me into the bathroom. I'm still shocked at his strength to just move me around like I weigh nothing.

My thoughts shift as he steps into the tub and lowers both of us into the water. It's hot, and burns my skin slightly, but feels glorious with each second that passes. Positioning us just like last time, he takes the spot behind me and pulls my back flush to his chest.

Unable to even hold up my head, it bobs back, rolling back onto his shoulder. My hair sticks to his sweaty chest.

"I'm sorry if I was too rough with you. I didn't mean to be. I just—I thought I lost you and something overtook me. It won't happen again," he murmurs into my hair. His lips feel like heaven, and I want to do it all over again.

"You scared me for a moment, but mostly because I didn't know what you were doing. Then—I don't know, I started to like it, and by the end, it was great," I say shyly. I feel weird admitting that to him...or myself, for that matter.

What does that say about me?

"Is it weird I liked it?"

"No, not at all. A lot of girls like it rough."

His words make me cringe and think about what Damon said yesterday.

Is that what he wants? A girl who likes it rough, who wants to be manhandled? Though I liked it, I don't think I'd want to do it like that all the time. My thoughts swirl crazily now. I feel jealous and don't really understand why. I know I shouldn't be jealous of the girls Hero slept with before he even knew me, but I can't help how I feel.

"Is that what you want?" I ask him. I need to know more now, after experiencing his dominant side. "Do you like to be rough with me? Is that what you'd want all the time?"

I can feel him shift nervously behind me as his body stiffens uncomfortably. He gives me an answer before he even starts speaking, and that hurts. It really hurts. "I do, but I don't want to hurt you...ever. I'm scared of losing you, Elyse. I'm terrified of hurting you or scaring you, and if me being rough does either of those things, I'll just learn to deal with it."

What does deal with it mean?

Is he just not going to be satisfied, or is he going to satisfy himself? Or maybe he'll find someone else who does like it that way to get him off. Every impossibly bad scenario runs through my mind.

I don't say anything for a long moment. I think Hero realizes something is wrong because he tips my head back and angles me so he can reach my lips. He kisses me so fiercely, I can't even remember my own name. When he pulls away, I'm breathless and a goopy mess of nothing.

"I know you're probably thinking the worst things possible...wondering if I'll keep you. If I'll find someone else to satisfy my needs."

My breath hitches at the very thought. Hero grips me by the chin, forcing me to look into his soft green eyes. His touch makes me shiver, and I feel at home in his arms. If I ever lost him, if he ever told me he didn't really want me anymore or tossed me away...

I'm not sure what I'd do.

He continues, refusing to let me say a single word. "There's a difference between the man Damon told you about yesterday and the man holding you right now, the man who gives you pleasure like you've never felt before."

"Yeah, and what is that difference?" I ask nervously, afraid of the answer I might receive.

He smirks, two perfect dimples appearing on his face.

"I'm in love now. In. Fucking. Love. With you. I'd never risk that for some piece of ass. I'd never jump ship because you don't want to do something. You're mine, Elyse, until the day you stop breathing, and if you think you can get rid of me that easily, then you're in for the ride of your life."

His words calm me, and the possessive look in his eyes proves he isn't lying. That's all I need to hear to know Hero wants me and only me.

I kiss him again, knowing he'll always protect me—always love me.

19

ero

THE WEEKS PASS, all seeming to blend into one. Nothing has changed. Elyse is still staying with me and remains by my side day and night.

I've even been taking her with me on drops, unable to bring myself to a level where I feel comfortable leaving her alone at the house. And to make matters worse, she has been asking to go back to classes. I don't want to be a bastard, the asshole who is over protective or possessive as hell, but this is how it needs to be right now.

Until I know she's absolutely safe, secure, and no one is after her, she won't be attending classes. I don't care how much she fights me on it.

"Get dressed, babe. We've got to meet someone." I don't ever tell her what exactly we are doing, or who we're meeting. Not because I don't trust her, but because if I were to ever get caught, she technically wouldn't be lying to the cops when she said she didn't know what was going on.

"Okay." She gets off the couch, without questioning me even a little bit.

I watch her walk into our bedroom and over to the dresser holding most of her clothes. I can't pull my gaze from her. The way the fabric covers her perfectly sculpted body, those hips I love to dig my fingers into while I'm fucking her, and her curves that give me enough cushion...enough to hold onto.

Fuck, I can feel myself getting hard, and all she's doing is putting clothes on. Damn, everything she does is sexy to me.

I'm so enamored by her getting dressed, I almost forget to get dressed myself. After quickly pulling on my own clothing, we head out the door. Like the gentleman I am, I hold Elyse's door open for her and let her get in the car before I get into the driver's side.

"Where are we going?"

"Meeting a friend at the football field. I just need to give him something. Then maybe we can go out for dinner or something?" We've been cooped up in the house the last couple days, maybe a night out is what we need.

"I'd like that." She gives me the most gorgeous smile, making my heart skip two beats.

It doesn't take us long to get to the football field. When I pull up to the field, I spot Gunner's car parked at the far end of the lot.

As I get closer, I see he is not inside. Instead, there's a girl leaning up against the hood. Strange. It isn't normal for Gunner to have a girl with him.

I take the spot next to him and cut the engine.

"Just sit tight for a minute. I've got to see where he is."

Getting out of the car, I feel myself getting pissed off. I told him what time to meet me, and I expect him to be here. Everyone knows you don't make your dealer wait.

The girl sitting on his car straightens. She eyes me nervously, a lot like Elyse did when I first met her.

"Where is Gunner?" I growl, a little harsher than necessary. She flinches at my tone, and I feel a little bad for acting like an ass.

It's not her fault he's not here.

"He—He went to the locker room, I-I think. He said he'd be right back," she tells me with a shaky voice.

The passenger door of my car opens, and Elyse climbs out.

Fucking Christ.

"What are you doing?" she yells at me, like she's accusing me of a crime, her eyes narrowing. "Don't you see you are scaring her?"

I inhale a calming breath, but it doesn't really help, not with Gunner not being here. All I want is to finish up business and take my girl out for dinner, how fucking hard is that?

Elyse stomps across the parking lot and goes to stand next to the girl. She holds her hand out as if she's offering a hand shake. "Hi, I'm Elyse. Don't mind him. He can be a little grumpy sometimes, but once you get to know him, he becomes a sweetie."

"Elyse!" The last thing I need is her making customers think I'm weak. When you're weak, you get taken advantage of.

The girl visibly relaxes with Elyse's friendly gesture. In fact, she takes her extended hand and shakes it. "Hi, I'm Lily." She gives Elyse a soft smile, and I can easily see them becoming friends.

Out the corner of my eye, I see Gunner walking out of the locker rooms. As soon as he sees me, he picks up speed, almost running straight toward us. Jocks…they're always buying some shit. Today's pick is molly. I hope like hell he's not using it on the girl with him tonight. Then again, it's none of my fucking business. I'm the dealer. Not a guidance counselor.

"I'm sorry, man," he apologizes once in earshot.

"Don't ever make me wait again," I say through my teeth. I don't want to get violent, especially with Elyse here, but the job means I have to get my hands dirty sometimes. And this might be one of those times. "Elyse, get back in the car," I order, and by some fucking miracle, she listens to me without question. She gives Lily a small wave as I walk to the trunk of the car and pop it open to get out the package he orders. He slips me a wad of cash without me asking for it, and I hand him what he paid for.

"See you next time." I get back into the car, glad this is all over with. I hate doing these drops. I hate working for Damon. And more than anything, I hate bringing Elyse out to do bad shit when she's the purest fucking thing in my life. Gunner gives me a nod as I get back in my car and race out of the parking lot as if I can't get away from the shit fast enough.

Elyse fumbles with her seatbelt, my reckless driving throwing her all over the car. She's got a worried look on her face, and I wonder what she thinks of me doing all this shit. She could have someone better—hell, she deserves better. But I'm selfish...too selfish to let her go and be with someone else.

"Where are we going?" she questions cautiously.

My grip on the steering wheel tightens, my muscles bunching together. Fuck, why was I given an angel when God knows I'm the fucking devil in disguise? "Wherever you want, baby," I grit out, refusing to take my shit attitude out on her. I've been treading lightly lately, not wanting to set her off.

The day I lost it and took her roughly, I could've sworn I'd saw some type of fear in her dazzling blue eyes. After seeing it, I never want to see again. Especially not when she looks at me. Then, during the bath, the way she looked at me and the things she asked me...

Like I'd ever fucking give her up for some whore I could fuck however I want. Yeah, no. Elyse is worth cherishing, worth protecting and making love to. She is what I want, what I always want.

"Can we go to Chips?"

The smile she gives me lessens the tension building deep inside me. I can't help but smile back at her. It's a tight smile, but a smile nonetheless.

"I want a strawberry shake, double cheeseburger, and french fries."

I chuckle. "Wow, that's a lot of food, baby. Where you putting all that?"

Elyse shrugs. "I don't know, but if I keep eating the way you're feeding me, I'll be gaining weight in no time. I hope you'll still love me when I'm fat."

I know Elyse thinks she's not good enough. I think part of that stems from her family always telling her how worthless she is. And then the things Damon said to her that night at Night Shift didn't help her confidence.

The opposite took place. It broke her down, made her insecure, but fuck, how could she not know how perfect she is?

Silence settles between us, her eyes moving over the scenery as I drive. I take my hand and place it on her knee, squeezing it gently. Her gaze drops down to it, and she places her tiny hand on top of mine.

When we pull into Chips, I order our food and pay. It's a little drive-in place that has the best handmade shakes in town.

Elyse takes hers and licks the whipped cream off the top. The move is so seductive, my cock hardens at the image before me. Then, her eyes drift closed, and she moans.

Jesus, woman.

"Growing up, my parents never let us have ice cream or cake," Elyse confesses, her eyes back open as she places a big spoonful of strawberry shake into her mouth.

"Wait, you never had cake and ice cream? For your birthday?" For some reason, this angers me.

She shakes her head, swallowing the food in her mouth before speaking. "Nope. We don't celebrate birthdays or holidays. We go to church. That was our exploration outside of the home for the week. The women stay in the house, cooking, cleaning, and taking care of the children."

"You left the house once a week? What the fuck?" I shake my head in disbelief. "Now I feel bad about not slugging your dad in the face when I had the chance." I should've. I should've knocked him right the fuck out.

Elyse giggles, her eyes sparkling, her hair flowing in the wind as a light breeze blows through the rolled down windows. "It's okay. I got out. I feel bad for the rest of my siblings, though." She frowns.

"Was it hard leaving them behind?" I ask, unsure why I want to know. Our pasts don't matter, not really, but knowing where Elyse came from helps me understand her better. She's so sweet and innocent and gives everyone the benefit of the doubt. But only because she doesn't know better, and I finally get a glimpse of why.

"A couple of them I miss..." She shoves a fry into her shake, then into her mouth. "But most of them hated me when they found out our parents were letting me go to college. And the only reason I think they let me go was because they knew I'd do it anyway, even if they didn't want me to. I've always been kind of the troublemaker, did what I wanted and got the belt a couple times." She pauses briefly.

The idea of someone spanking her, touching her porcelain skin...yeah, it makes me want to kill.

"This way, it made it look more like they were approving even though it's painfully obvious they weren't."

That makes me straight up laugh. "You were the troublemaker of the family?"

"Yeah, I know, shocking. But being the youngest has its perks." She winks.

It's so adorable, I want to kiss her, but don't. Instead, I let her continue to eat. "Is that where you went that morning? To see your parents?" I take a bite of my own burger, mainly because I look like a total idiot sitting here watching her eat while I ask a million and one questions.

Elyse nods, her eyes professing how sorry she is...*still*. Fucking Christ, this girl doesn't let anything go.

"My mom said she had something to tell me, something she couldn't tell me over the phone." She rolls her eyes. "But like always, it was just another stunt to get me to come home. This time, though, she blew it. I don't plan on talking to either of my parents ever again."

"I'm glad you feel that way. Honestly, I wouldn't want you to. Trust me, sometimes you're better off cutting your parents out of your life." Just thinking about the scumbag of a father I have makes me lose my appetite. He's not even worth the thinking space inside my head.

"You sound like you're talking from experience."

"Nothing gets by you, detective." I think about changing the subject, so I don't have to talk about him, but Elyse just shared something about her family and now I feel obligated to do the same. That's what normal couples do, right? They share things, even stuff they don't want to talk about with anybody else. "My mom was the sweetest person you could ever meet, but she had a talent for picking the biggest assholes. She married my dad right after high school. He got her pregnant before she even graduated. I think they might have gotten married just because of it. Anyway, he started drinking, cheating, and abusing her when I was just a baby. My mom was scared of leaving him and raising me on her own, so she just let it happen. My grandma told me years later it wasn't until he put his hand on me that my mom got up and left his ass. Of course, the guys she dated after weren't much better. Like I said, she had a talent."

"I'm so sorry. Is your grandma still alive?"

I can tell Elyse feels bad for me, but there isn't any point in it. I don't want her pity. "No. She died a year before my mom did." Elyse frowns even more, and I hate the look on her face. I want her smiles, always.

"I'm really sorry, Hero." She places her hand on my knee.

I welcome the warmth of her touch.

"What about your dad? Is he still alive?"

The subject of my father stings and leaves me feeling angry and disappointed. "Unfortunately, yes. I wish the fucker would die, but that'll never happen." No, god no, why take a piece of shit junkie who's wasting their life when you can take a caring mother from her son?

Elyse seems a bit wary, her eyes bleeding into mine. "You don't really mean that, do you?"

I swallow down some of the anger I was about to unleash. Her question pisses me right off. "You can't be serious," I growl.

Elyse's eyes widen with confusion.

"He abused my mother and me. He's the reason my mother married my now dead stepfather..." I'm seething. My entire night is ruined, and all because of him. "You know, Elyse, you're naive to the world. You believe everyone has some type of good in them. I get that." I clench my jaw. "But he doesn't deserve an ounce of space in our conversation. He doesn't deserve anything but a bullet in the head." I let the words hang in the air, my eyes refusing to meet Elyse's. This is where we are not alike—the part of us that would always remain different. Elyse sees the world as her oyster.

I see it as something that could destroy you because despite what Elyse believes, there are more bad people than good in the world.

"I'm sorry you feel that way. I don't want a relationship with my parents anymore, but I can't imagine ever wishing they were dead."

"Let's just go home and forget about this conversation, okay?" This was supposed to be a fun date, but it turned into a shitshow as soon as my dad was mentioned.

Way to ruin everything, Dad.

20

lyse

"Come here." Hero's voice is soft, his green eyes kind, and the way he's looking at me has my body turning into melted butter.

I walk across the living room slowly, my hips swaying, a sultry smile on my lips. "What if I don't want to come over there?" I bat my eyes, playing hard to get. I like seeing Hero smile and laugh. It reminds me there is more to him than what he lets the world see, and right now, he's smiling like he never has before, amusement twinkling in his eyes.

He's happy. If I could bottle up this moment and save it, I would.

My chest heaves as his pink tongue darts out over his bottom lip, a playful grin pulling at his lips. "Then I guess I'll have to bring you over here myself."

I wiggle my eyebrows and make a move toward the kitchen, but I know before I even take a step that I'm not fast enough to get away from him. At six-foot-three, Hero could eat up the distance between us like it's nothing.

In seconds, he has me in his arms, his lips on mine, his hand tangled in my hair as he drags me back with him in the direction of the couch. I'd let our slight argument from the night before go. There's no point in fighting with him on something he's set in his ways about.

"I want you," he murmurs into my ear, his teeth raking against the sensitive lobe.

I arch into his touch. My panties are already drenched, my need for him all-consuming. I let him make quick work of my clothing while I grasp his pants and t-shirt, undressing him just as hastily.

"Come sit on my lap, straddle me," he instructs, sitting back on the couch. Taking my hand, he pulls me forward. "I want you to sit on my dick and ride me. You're in control today. Use me as you please. Take what you want, baby."

Not knowing how to do any of that, I give him a confused and apprehensive look. Familiar doubt fills my mind faster than I can handle. I don't know if I can be what he wants me to be. "I don't know how to."

"Don't worry, babe. Just go with it. Trust me and trust yourself. Your body knows how to move all by itself." He sounds confident enough for us both.

I try to draw on that confidence as I lower myself onto him. His cock is intimidating as hell, even more so with the little barbell at the end of it. I've felt it many times inside me, but I'd never watched it slide into me.

Hero growls softly as his hard length enters my soaking wet pussy with ease. I moan when he hits a new spot deep inside me. This position feels different, deeper, fuller.

"That's it...god, you feel so good."

I don't even realize I'm moving until he points it out. My hips rock into him all on their own. It feels so incredibly good, and every move drives me higher. I start rolling my hips more and more, my pelvis grinding into him, claiming him. Hero puts his hands on either side of them, moving me gently, guiding me to go faster. The pace is relentless, but it's also what I need. He releases his hold on my hips suddenly, as if he remembers I'm the one who's supposed to be in control.

Lifting his arms, he interlaces his fingers and puts them behind his head as a form of control.

I smile, loving that he's letting me run the show instead of him. My own hands press against his chiseled chest for support. He's so warm beneath my touch, his body reacting to mine with every movement I make. I roll my hips even more, swiveling them, grinding myself into him, and I'm rewarded with a deep groan.

Hero's eyes close, and his head leans back. "Fuck..." he hisses out.

It's barely audible, but I hear it and take that as encouragement I must be doing this the right way.

Moving harder and faster, I get into a rhythm, feeling my own peak forming deep down inside my core. I'm panting so hard, I'm starting to sound like I'm running a marathon. Sweat forms against my brow as I lean into Hero, pressing a kiss to his lips.

He's so caught up in the bliss of it all, he gives me a sloppy one, which only makes me smile more.

My nails dig deep into Hero's skin as I'm on the verge of losing control. The sound of my ass slapping against his thighs fills the room. My body vibrating, my legs shaking, my mind thinking of only this moment between us.

When I started out, I was more worried about pleasing Hero, but somewhere along the way, it became about me. Now, I grind into him, chasing my own orgasm. The tip of his cock presses against something wild inside of me. The pleasure owns me. Moving in just the right spot, at the right speed for myself. I let that selfishness take over and do what Hero said. I use him and take him as I please, do what I want with him. The fact that he's given me this intensifies everything...every emotion is magnified.

My head falls back, and my eyes squeeze shut as my whole body explodes. My womb flutters, literally flutters, like it has a damn heartbeat of its own, and I'm pretty sure I scream Hero's name, but that might have been inside my head. My release is so strong, I can't think clearly. Everything is floating, and my body feels like it's not even in this world anymore.

When my mind returns to the present, I lean forward and put both of my hands on either side of Hero's face, pressing my still trembling lips to his.

"That was the hottest fucking thing I've ever seen," he tells me after I peel my lips away and rest my head on his shoulder.

It takes me a few moments to realize he didn't come yet, his still rock-hard cock inside me.

I sit up and grip onto his shoulders. As I start moving my hips again, my still overly sensitive clit rubs against him with every swivel, making me hiss out.

His arms come around my back, holding me tightly to him. This time, he does guide my movements on top of him. Gripping onto my hips a little tighter, he takes even more control. "Is this okay?" he whispers.

"Yes. It's your turn now, to use me as you please..."

At my words, a primal grunt rumbles from his chest, and his grip tightens almost painfully. He moves me with the thrust of his hips, driving into me impossibly deep. I bite into the flesh on his shoulder so I won't scream and scare half the neighborhood.

How deep he is combined with the constant friction against my clit draws yet another orgasm out of me. My walls clench around his dick, setting off his own release. He pulls me in one last time before he stills. Both of our bodies are covered in sweat, making every movement between us feel slimy. Still, I relish in the feeling of his skin against mine. Our combined smells mix together, and I want to stay like this forever...

Hell, who knows, maybe if I knew sex was this good, I would've tossed my v-card out the window a long time ago. "We need a shower, but I—can't move." Even saying the words is a struggle. *Breathing* is a struggle.

Hero chuckles. "Give me a minute, and I'll carry you."

Just as promised, a minute later, he picks me up and carries me into the bathroom. Hero turns on the shower and makes sure it's the perfect temperature before stepping into it with me. He sets my feet down onto the ground, steadying me before removing his hand from my hip.

Once I have my footing, he washes me from head to toe, his touch gentle, then shampoos and conditions my hair before he washes himself. I feel like a damn princess.

When we step out, he wraps me up in a large towel and takes me into the bedroom.

Taking advantage of his good mood, I decide now is the perfect time to bring up me wanting more freedom. "Hero, I want to go back to my classes, to tutoring." I keep my voice strong. There...like ripping off a Band-Aid, quick and pain free, I spit the words out.

"No."

I wait for him to say something else, but he just gets dressed, as if that's all he is going to say to that.

"Just no?" I place my hands on my hips, not quite understanding what he is saying. *No?* Like he can tell me what I can and cannot do?

"I already told you. You are not going to leave my side until I find whoever is watching you. The answer is still no and will remain no until I find the person I'm looking for...." He pauses, his eyes meeting mine, an unsaid promise shining back at me.

"And I won't change my mind. If I were you, I would just stop asking."

I cannot help but roll my eyes. "Hero, I left my family to be free. I left so I could make my own decisions and not have people tell me what is best for me. I didn't leave one prison to become trapped in another. Plus, we don't even know if this person is real. I just felt like someone was watching me, just like you used to. Maybe I was just being paranoid."

"Don't compare me to your parents. I'm doing this to protect you, not harm you." He completely ignores my other comment.

I laugh, but nothing about this conversation is funny. "Funny, because that's exactly what they used to say."

Hero's features darken. "I don't care what you think, or say, you are not going."

I tell myself to tread lightly, not to push him over the edge, but it's been two weeks and nothing bad has happened. I can't help but fear that maybe Hero is just trying to keep me here with him, so I dig deep inside myself and find my lady balls. "Hero, I'm not asking you. I'm telling you! I'm going back to class. If you don't like it, then I'm moving back in with Tasha. I won't be controlled, and I won't trade one prison for another."

I see the moment he snaps in his eyes. Disappointment and hurt seeping through his, furious gaze.

It pierces through my heart, but I can't let him gain control over me, not like this. I want to have a normal life and I can't hide out here forever.

I can have Hero and still be a normal college kid, right?

"Fine then, go! Go back to your precious classes. Go be a tutor for pennies, and don't forget to get drugged and raped at parties between all your studying." He pulls his shirt on and storms out the door.

I think about stopping him, but decide to let him cool off first. I know he didn't mean what he said, but that doesn't make his words hurt any less.

When I hear the front door slam a moment later, sadness seeps into my bones. That's when the first tear rolls down my cheek. While I'm getting myself dressed, I tell myself I did the right thing. I need to make him understand where I stand. I can't let him make all the decisions in my life. After I'm fully dressed, I decide I need to spend some time with a friend today.

Tasha may still be mad at me for moving in with Hero, but I'm certain she would meet me if I asked her to. Getting my phone out, I send her a quick text asking if she wants to meet for coffee after I talk to the administration people about making up the classes I've missed.

She returns my message almost immediately, and I sigh in relief. At least I didn't lose the one and only friend I've made. I slip into my flats and stick my phone into my backpack. I sling it over my shoulder and head out the door. I don't lock it, though. I don't know when Hero will be home and I don't want to be locked out.

Cool, fresh air hits me as soon as I step outside. As I walk along the sidewalk, I realize this is the first time in weeks I've been outside on my own.

Which makes me happy and slightly sad, because truthfully, I miss Hero.

Pushing the unwanted feelings aside, I concentrate on the freedom I fought so hard for today and walk myself right up to the administrative building.

I barely make it halfway up the block when the feeling of being watched creeps up on me. The hair on the back of my neck stands up, alerting me. Looking around anxiously, I tell myself it's nothing. Maybe it's just Hero trying to scare me. It wouldn't really surprise me.

Letting my backpack fall off my shoulder, I swing it around so I can take my phone out. I'm just going to call Hero and tell him where I am just in case. I unlock my phone and scroll down to Hero's name. My fingers move nervously across the screen. Just as I'm about to press the call button, my arms break out into goosebumps and the air shifts around me.

Something's wrong. Something is very wrong.

I'm not quick enough to turn around and face my attacker. Someone large and strong grabs me from behind and covers my mouth with a white cloth. I panic as my legs thrash. My body surges with a need to run and escape. My fingers dig into my attacker's arms, but it's no use my vision starts to blur, and my grip loosens.

A sickening laugh fills my ears. It sounds far away, but close at the same time. I suck in a deep breath to scream, but the words are muffled. No one can hear me. I feel myself drifting further and further away from this world.

The last thought I have before everything turns black is I hope I can tell Hero how sorry I am for not believing him.

21

ero

The beer goes down smoother than I anticipated. Then again, when you're pissed off at the entire world and you need an outlet other than fucking, it's going to.

The petite bartender with fake boobs slides me another beer as if she can read my mind. "I get off in an hour if you want to drink some free beers at my place." She bats her eyelashes at me.

Ha. As if there was a fucking chance in hell I'd take her up on the offer. "No thanks. I like spending nine bucks for a beer at a strip club."

She gives me an eyeroll and walks back down to the other side of the bar, probably on a mission to find her next one-night stand. I can't hold it against her, though. She doesn't know the organ beating in my chest isn't my own anymore.

Damon takes the seat beside me and slaps a hand on my shoulder. "Did you see the new girl on the stage?"

I fist the beer bottle in my hand hard enough to break it.

He leans in closer, his voice a whisper. "That one likes it rough. She'll give you exactly what you want and need. You want me to send her to the backroom to meet you?"

I have to remind myself he means well in his own fucked-up Damon way. That doesn't mean I don't want to smash his face in any less. "No, I don't want to fuck your stripper or strippers." I sigh. Explaining this to him is going to eat up most of my patience. "I know the concept is foreign to you, so I don't know how I can make you understand it, but I love Elyse."

Anger festers. I love her, even though she's the biggest pain in my ass. Even though she tests me and pushes my buttons—fuck, I love her.

Damon's eyes go wide. He has no fucking idea what I'm talking about. I realize this would be like trying to explain algebra to a toddler.

"Okay...well, I'll be in my office if you change your mind."

I shake my head, completely dumbfounded at his response, and watch him walk through the place like he's in a hurry.

All right, so he doesn't really care to hear about things with Elyse. He disappears to the back office, and I continue my crusade to drink the entire place out of beer. But as I do so, my thoughts change. The feelings I've pushed down rise to the surface.

I come to terms with the fact that I shouldn't have walked away. I should've fucking stayed at the house, tried to talk to her about everything, tried to reason with her and explain how her safety is my greatest priority.

My anger toward Elyse shifts and now I'm madder at myself than I was at her in the first damn place. I'm so mad at myself, I consider starting a fight with one of the assholes in this place just so I can get my ass kicked.

Music blasts through the speakers, making my head pound. I down the rest of my beer and stand from the bar stool. I nearly collapse against the bar, my feet not quite ready to carry me. I know I need to get home to Elyse, but I'm not sure how I'm going to do that. Forcing myself upright, I drunkenly walk toward Damon's office.

Maybe he can give me a ride home.

As I get closer to his office, the voices get louder. Damon's not alone. I lean closer to the door so I can hear them without looking conspicuous. In my mind, I'm doing a good job. Sober me would probably say I'm not.

"You will listen to me, Kiera, or you will die. This world isn't the same as yours. You're walking into a fucking nightmare. One wrong move in this world will get you killed. Do you understand me?"

Kiera? I can't remember anyone named Kiera. In fact, I can't remember the last time Damon let a woman into his office.

"Just tell me what happened to him," Kiera pleads, her voice tiny, just like my Elyse's.

"First rule, don't ask questions. That's exactly the kind of thing I'm talking about. Questions like that will get you killed. Just keep your mouth shut and do what I say, otherwise I'll find another job for you, and you don't really look like the sucking cock type."

I hear a sob, and curiosity finally gets the better of me. I knock three times in quick succession before opening it without bothering to wait for his invite to come inside.

He looks furious for a moment, then sees it's me and sighs. "Changed your mind about the girl I offered?" Of course, everything is about business with this man.

"No, I came to ask you for a ride home," I slur, almost collapsing into the chair at the front of his desk. My eyes move around the room as it spins.

This is not fucking good.

"You think going home to your girl like this is a good idea?"

"No, but any other idea is shit too. Doesn't matter when I go home, my ass is still going to be chewed." My eyes gain enough focus and to land on the mystery woman.

She's tiny, maybe five-foot, one hundred and twenty pounds. Her hair is a dark auburn, and her eyes are wide and full of fear. She looks like she's been caught in a trap with no way out.

"How about you crash at my place tonight? I've got something at home that will calm you down a bit without making you puke your guts out in the morning."

"Sure, let's go. I don't know how much longer my legs will work." I slowly get up from the chair, my entire body swaying as the contents in my stomach slosh from one side to the other.

How much beer did I drink?

Damon looks at the girl for a moment, then back to me before getting up and walking past me. "Let's go, Kiera. Get your shit, you're coming with me."

She nervously grabs something next to the couch and gets up, her legs just as unsteady as mine.

I can't believe my eyes when she starts following Daman like a lost puppy. Is he taking her to his place? Who is this girl? I must be way more drunk than I thought. My mind has to be playing tricks on me. There is no way in hell Damon is bringing her back to his house, or even letting her ride in his car.

I save the millions of questions for later and manage to follow Damon out to his car. Opening the door, I nearly fall on my ass as I slip into the passenger side. A whimper from the back seat catches my attention.

"How drunk am I?" I lean over and ask Damon.

He doesn't look like he's in the mood for my bullshit, but most days, I'm not in the mood for his, so he can deal. "Pretty fucking drunk."

I nod, as if I understand completely. "Okay, good. Because I could've sworn there was a chick in the backseat of your car."

Damon shakes his head, and if I didn't know better, I'd say a small smile appears on his lips. But I do know better. Nothing makes him smile. Nothing but money and power.

By the time we get to his place, I am only an eight on the drunk scale. I can walk a little straighter and talk just a tad clearer.

"Go to the guest room and lock the door behind you," he orders to the girl I keep forgetting exists.

She scurries away, disappearing into the night.

I follow Damon into his living room and sink onto the comfortable leather couch.

He gets out a small metal case from his back pocket and flips it open, revealing three neatly rolled joints. Taking the seat next to me, he pulls a lighter out of his other pocket and lights up one of the joints.

The sweet smell of weed fills my nostrils as Damon breathes out a thick cloud of smoke. He takes two more drags before handing it to me. Greedily, I take a drag, instantly calming.

"So, you really are in love with that girl," Damon says, like it just now sunk into his brain.

"So fucking much, it hurts. I keep fucking up, but I can't help it. She pushes all my buttons, good and bad. It's driving me insane."

Damon nods as if he suddenly knows what I'm talking about, but he doesn't understand—he has no fucking clue.

WHEN I WAKE UP, my head feels like it's stuffed with cotton and my eyes feel like someone poured sand in them. Everything hurts...every damn thing.

I wish someone would make that ringing noise stop. The high pitch sound is like a jackhammer to my brain. Prying my extremely dry eyes open, I try to take in my unfamiliar surroundings and make sense of it. It takes me a moment to realize I'm at Damon's, then another to realize the annoying ringing is coming from my phone.

With my throat just as dry as my eyes, I answer the phone. My voice sounds like its coming from an eighty-year-old chain smoker. "Hello?"

"Um, hey...Hero?" A timid voice filters through the phone.

"Yeah?" I look at the screen. It's a number I don't recognize. "Who is this?"

"It's Tasha."

Tasha? Why the hell is she calling me?

"I was just wondering if you know where Elyse is. She was supposed to meet me for coffee yesterday and she never showed. I called her phone a million times, but it went to voicemail. I want to make sure she's okay."

In less than a second, I am wide awake, my head as clear as ever.

"When...? When did she call and what time were you supposed to meet?" I need all the information I can get. I'm already up and putting my shoes on, trying to find my keys. *Shit! My car is still at the club.*

I run down the hallway to Damon's bedroom, not bothering to knock before I storm in. "Damon, get up! I need you to drive me to my car...now!"

He sits up in the bed, staring at me like I've just lost my mind. "Are you serious?"

"I'm not fucking with you, get the fuck up and dressed. Elyse is missing."

He grunts in annoyance, but gets up and throws on some clothes.

I don't have the patience to stand around and wait, so I rush outside, nearly running over the girl from last night in the hallway. I don't pay her an ounce of attention. I can't, not when my thoughts are on finding Elyse.

I can't fucking believe I left her alone...that I let her have her way out of anger. I clench my fists, wanting to punch myself in the face.

We hop in the car, and Damon speeds off down his driveway. His phone rings shortly after we're on the road. "What?" he growls before he goes silent for a moment, listening to the person on the other end. "Shit! Meet me at the club, right now!" He hangs up and floors it.

My body slams back into the seat at the force.

"That was one of my bookies. He was supposed to pick up cash this morning, but the guy couldn't pay. They were about to break some bones when the guy told them he could pay us back double of what he owed in the next few days..." He pauses like he doesn't want to tell me the next part.

I know it's going to be bad. I brace myself for the worst. Deep down, I know it has to do with Elyse. "Spit it out, Damon." I don't even recognize my voice. I feel myself disconnecting from the world, my thoughts on one singular thing: getting Elyse back.

"He said he kidnapped a girl last night and he was going to get ransom money for her soon. Didn't say who he kidnapped, but I'm sure you can put the pieces together."

I can't breathe. Preparing myself and actually hearing him say it are two very different things. This is real, and it's all my fucking fault.

"Listen, Hero, this is good. You might not see it this way now, but he wants money, so he won't hurt her, and we know who he is. We'll find her..."

I hear the words, but they're just jumbled up words with no meaning. But the one thing Damon says does ring out inside my head. *We will find her.* When we do, I'll take the bastard's life for touching what is mine.

Damon breaks every speed limit on the way to the club, but we're still not going fast enough. The thought of Elyse scared and hurt somewhere guts me, ripping my insides apart. If something happens to her, I will never forgive myself.

When we finally pull up to the club, someone is waiting at the back entrance. I pray to god it's the guy who has information for us. I throw open the door and get out before Damon even puts the car in park. "What do you know? Tell me everything! Where the fuck is she?" I shout, grabbing two fistfuls of the unknown man's shirt. I slam him against the brick exterior wall. I don't care about anyone but Elyse. If I have to, I'll kill the fucker in front of me to get the information I need out of him.

"Calm down, man!" He shakes me off.

I don't let him up. I keep him pressed against the wall.

"I'll tell you everything I know. Just let me up…"

Damon appears beside us, nodding at the guy. "Did he tell you anything else about the girl and where he took her? What's the guy's name?"

I shove the guy against the wall and take a step back. My thoughts are muddled, my body filled to the brim with tension. I have to find her—I have to. I clench my jaw and slam my fist into the brick wall, over and over again, until warm blood drips down my hand.

"He didn't say where he took her. We tried to follow him, but he got away. I don't know the guy's full name, but he goes by the nickname of Rocky."

Something inside me snaps. It awakens that feeling of death and floods my veins. "No fucking way!" I can't believe my ears. It can't be him.

"You know the guy he's talking about?" Damon eyes me curiously. He seems slightly afraid of me, and that only sets me off more.

"Oh yeah, I fucking know him all right."

I'm seething—hanging right on the edge of insanity, ready to fucking jump off into the deep end.

22

lyse

As soon as I come to, I know something is very wrong. My head throbs, my stomach churns, and my vision is blurry. I try to organize my thoughts, make sense of everything, but nothing fits like it's supposed to.

With a stiff neck, I turn my head to take in my surroundings.

I'm in some kind of basement. Different smells assault me, but I can't place them. The room smells like mildew and dirt.

I try to move my arms, quickly realizing I can't. Panic grips me like a hand closing in around my throat. My ass throbs as if I've been sitting for hours. I try to push from my sitting position, but can't. My eyes slip down over my body to see a thin rope wrapped around my ankles and calves. I realize my hands are tied as well as I try and flex them.

"Hello?" I barely recognize the raspy voice coming out of

me. My throat is so unbelievably dry, and my lips are painfully cracked.

The door at the top of the stairs creaks open, throwing rays of sunshine down the steps. Heavy footsteps follow, and every single one makes my stomach twist a little bit more. I'm so scared, my whole body is tremor in fear.

I try to remember how I got here, but my thoughts are fuzzy, as if I've been drugged. The man who kidnapped me comes into view. My heart beats so hard, I'm worried I may have a heart attack.

My eyes take in my attacker. He is a big guy with broad shoulders and midnight black hair. As he comes closer, I see a sickening smile on his face.

"I'm so glad you are finally up, princess." His voice is cruel and as dark as his features.

"Who are you and what do you want?" I ask, my voice so jittery, I'm surprised the words come out at all.

"I've been trying to get my hands on you for a while now." He reaches a meaty hand up to my face.

I cringe, not wanting him to touch me. I try to pull away, but there's no room for me to move.

The look in his dark gaze is filled with excitement, longing. He drags his rough knuckle down my cheek. "I'd say you are worth the wait. So pretty...pure. I understand why Jonathan is so caught up in you."

Jonathan? I never heard anyone call Hero by his actual name. Confused, I look into my captor's eyes. Eyes that are somehow familiar, though I'm positive I've never met the man in front of me. Or have I? I take in the rest of his features. Black hair, strong jawline, and dark eyes.

Oh my god. Could he be...?

"A-Are y-you..." I stutter, my body quaking.

He must see recognition written all over my face because he finishes the sentence for me. "Jonathan's father?"

His smile widens, and I know I'm going to be sick.

"Why yes, I am dear old dad."

"Why are you doing this?" I croak. I don't understand. Why would he want to take me? Hurt me, hurt Hero? None of it makes sense. He has nothing to do with Hero and hasn't for years.

"I took you so my son would give me what belongs to me. His whore of a mother left everything to him. All the money, her car, the house we bought together. All of those things should have been mine, not his." His words flow from his mouth like venom, full of hate and resentment. "Then your parents came to me. I met them at that cute little church you all go to each Sunday. I saw the perfect opportunity and your stupid fucking parents played right into it." He laughs a humorless laugh. "The fucking dumbasses paid me to kidnap you. Now, I've got their money and I'm going to get a ransom for you on top of that."

My parents?

His words sink in, slow and painful. My parents hired him to kidnap me? This can't be happening. This must all be a bad dream I'm about to wake up from any minute now. I'll wake up and Hero will be lying next to me in the bed, telling me to calm down because it was nothing but a nightmare.

"We are going to take a little video for your boyfriend so he knows how serious I am about this." He fishes a phone out of his pocket and fumbles with it for a second before pointing it at my face. "Guess who I'm hanging out with? That's right, sweet Elyse. It doesn't look like she is having a good time, though. You might want to come get her real soon." He pans the phone back to himself, a sinister smile appearing on his face all over again. He looks evil, like he'd kill me without a second thought. "All you have to do to get her back is bring me a hundred grand in cash and I'll tell you where to pick her up." He looks past the phone into my eyes. "I need you to beg, Elyse. Beg him to come get you."

I've never been a violent person, but if my hands were free right now, I would shove that phone straight up his ass. I shake my head in defiance. He isn't going to get anything from me. I don't care about him or the money he wants. "He won't. He won't give you a dime. Just let me go and I'll go back to my parents. I won't tell anyone what happened. I swear," I plead with him, praying he's still a human with a heart.

"Wrong answer!" With his free hand, he slaps me across the face, making my head snap to the side. Pain throbs through my cheek as I hang off the side of the chair. I can't breathe, I can't think, I can't do anything but remain seated.

Pain-filled tears spring from my eyes. He doesn't give me time to say anything, or even move before he hits me again. This time, even harder than the last, making me cry out in pain.

"Beg, Elyse. Beg for your precious *Hero* to come save you."

I don't want to give him the satisfaction of winning, of having me beg, but when he strikes me a third time, my eyes shift closed and darkness clings to me. I'm about to pass out—one more slap and I'll be gone.

With the last shred of hope I have, I give into his demand, "Please…" I whimper, ashamed of my weakness.

"There you go, sweetie." He steps forward and grips my chin roughly.

My eyes swell. Blood trickles down from my nose. I don't even want to know the kind of damage that's been done.

Forcing me to look at him, he leans in. His breath smells of beer and cigarettes. "That wasn't so hard, was it?" He snickers to himself.

Tilting my head farther back, he angles the camera down to me. "If you don't want me to hurt this pretty face any more than I already have, you better come up with the money quickly. My patience is wearing thin, and I don't know how much longer I'll go without touching the more intimate parts of her." Hero's father doesn't even glance at me again.

He releases me with a shove and turns off the phone, stuffing it back into his pocket.

At his words, the bile rising in my throat fills my mouth and I bend over, vomiting all over the side of the chair. My hair clings to my sweaty forehead. I force air into my lungs, knowing if I don't, I will truly pass out. After hearing what the vile man before me just said, that's the last thing I want to do.

The evil bastard leans down, resting on the balls of his feet. "Now, why the fuck did you have to go and do that?" His face is a mask of fury.

Before I can even mutter a response, his clenched fist moves toward my face.

Moments later, everything goes black as my head rolls to the side.

My face throbs and one of my eyes is swollen so badly, I can barely open it. I don't know how long I've been here, but the grumbling of my belly signifies it's been awhile. Not that it would matter if the bastard brought me food. I don't think I could keep any of it down. Something to drink, to moisten the desert in my mouth, would be nice, though.

I keep drifting in and out of sleep from exhaustion, or maybe it's the aftermath of whatever drug he gave me. I dream about my mom being here. Her fingers touch my face gently, and I beg her for help, but she just turns around and walks back up the stairs. Sometimes, I'm not even sure if I'm awake or asleep. Maybe I'm trapped somewhere in between.

I'm about to pass out again when I hear footsteps above me. I strain, trying to hear better.

Multiple footsteps followed by voices. My heart pounds so hard, I can hear it in my ears. Someone is here—someone is here!

"Hello!" I try to scream, but only a low, broken voice comes out. It's so quiet, I can barely hear it myself.

"Help me!" I cry out. I try again and again, but I can't get the words to come out loud enough. My throat throbs with the effort. It hurts to mumble, let alone scream.

The creaking of the basement door opening startles me, and suddenly, I'm more scared than I was the first time I woke up here. What if he invited more bad people? What if they come down here to hurt me?

I struggle against the rope as it digs into my skin, rubbing at the already sensitive flesh. Tears sting my eyes. It's no use.

A pair of familiar boots come down the stairs first, and fear paralyzes me.

"Oh sweet, sweet Elyse, guess who is here to see you?" he coaxes, his gaze piercing mine, holding me in place.

Hero. Could it really be?

He came—he actually came...

A moment later, two more sets of legs appear behind him. My gaze moves away from him, and it doesn't take me long to realize who the people are. All three walk fully into the basement, stopping directly in front of me.

"Mom? Dad?" Disbelief drips from my lips. There is a moment where we all just look at each other. I blink slowly.

They can't really be here. If they were, they'd be helping me, right? That's what parents do. They help you—they protect you.

Not my parents, though. They just stand there and stare, like I'm a specter on display.

"This was not the deal we made," my father announces, sounding way less concerned than a father should seeing his daughter tied up, bruised, and locked in a basement. He says it more like he ordered a burger without pickles and they put the pickles on it anyway. Annoyance. Impatience. That's all I am to him.

My mom says nothing at all, which is worse, but not at all surprising.

"Help me," I whimper, begging my mother, pleading with her.

She looks at Hero's dad. "We'll take her home now."

Relief almost floods me. If they get me out of here, I can run away and back to Hero.

"No can do. I need your daughter for a little while longer. I told you, you could see her, but you can't take her. You saw her. You know she is alive. Now, leave." He gestures for them to head back up the stairs.

"We want to take her home now," my mother demands.

Hero's dad slips his hand into the back of his pockets and retrieves something, pointing it at my parents.

A gun, a knife maybe? I can't tell with my one eye.

My mom gasps, and my dad takes a step back, putting his hands up in the air.

"I said you can't take her right now. Don't make this harder than it needs to be. If it comes down to it, I'll fucking kill all of you." He motions the gun to each of us, pure death shining in his eyes. "Now, get the fuck out of here."

"Okay, okay, we are going." With his hands still in the air, my dad walks backwards toward the stairs. He stumbles over his feet and turns around to face the stairs once he touches them.

When my mother follows closely behind him, I lose all hope.

"No, Mom...please. Dad, don't leave me here. Please!" I cry out, but neither stops walking. Each step they take away from me pierces me straight in the heart.

The last thing I see is my mom mouthing, "Sorry," before they disappear upstairs.

I'll never forgive them for this. Never.

23

ero

I GRIP my phone so tightly in my hand, I'm close to snapping the damn thing. I will kill him. I will kill my father. I've watched the video ten times already. Part of me does it to look for clues that might help figure out where she is. The other reason is to torture myself.

This is all my fault. Every decision I made from the moment I stole our first kiss has led us here.

My sweet Elyse is in my father's clutches.

And I'm going to kill him for touching her. I don't care if I go back to prison for the rest of my life. I *will* kill him.

I already have the cash in hand, I just need him to call. I'll bring him the money, show it to him so he'll let her go, then slash his fucking throat

I sit on the couch, the same couch we fucked on. Elyse's scent swirls around me, haunting me. When this is all over…

I don't get a chance to finish my thought because a knock on my door drags me out of the daydream.

I get up and walk to the door, already feeling sorry for whoever is on the other side. I pull the door open, my hand fisting the knob so hard, I'm surprised I didn't rip it from the door itself. My eyes round when I find Elyse's parents standing there.

Her mom is crying, holding a tissue at the tip of her nose. Her eyes are bloodshot, and she looks like she's going to be sick.

"Can we come in, Hero?" her dad asks, catching me off guard with his tone.

What the fuck?

I'm a second away from slamming the door in their faces when her mother starts talking. "Please, Hero," she sniffles. "It's about Elyse. She's in trouble."

"I know she is. The question is how do you fucking know?" I snarl, on the verge of coming unhinged.

This doesn't make sense. Is my dad asking them for ransom too?

"We know where she is." Elyse's dad hands me a piece of paper.

If they didn't have my full attention before, they have it now. I unfold it immediately and read the address scribbled on it. "This is where she is? You're sure?" I don't even care how they got this information, or how they found out about it. All I care about is finding her—*now*. The thought of her remaining in his hands a second longer has me dashing out the door.

I push Elyse's mother out of the way and half knock over her dad. I couldn't care less, though. I have one thing on my mind.

I sprint to my car and climb into it. My tires squeal against the pavement as I haul ass out of the parking lot. I honk my horn and blow through every stop sign along the way. Staring at the address on the paper, I make certain I'm going the right way. Then I pull out my phone and call Damon.

I don't have time for pleasantries, so I give him the address and tell him to meet me there. Not that I'm going to need help with the killing part. It's the cleaning up I'll need Damon for.

I pull onto the street, searching for the house number. As soon as I spot it, I drive into the middle of the front lawn, cut the engine, and jump out of the car. I don't knock or check if the door is open.

Being in a *do things, asks questions later* kind of mood, I run toward it and kick it open as I go. My foot lands a few inches away from the door knob and the wood around it gives way with a loud crack. Another kick at the same spot and the door swings open.

As soon as I step over the threshold, I know my father is here. The house is vacant, not a single belonging, and though I can't explain how I know, I just do.

It's dark now, and there is no light filtering into the house. I see a shadow moving to my left and follow it. My first concern is finding Elyse.

And then I see him—another shadow.

"You've always been a fucking coward. Hiding in the dark, only brave enough to fight people half your size. Why don't you come out and be a man for once in your pathetic fucking life," I say as I creep through the house, my feet agile, my body ready for a fight, hoping I can draw him out.

"Oh, that's right. I forgot you can't be a man. Never have been one. You are nothing more than a fucking loser who can't keep a job or a woman. And you'll never be anything besides a lo—" my words are cut off as a body slams into me. I stagger to the side, but stay on my feet.

"Who do you think you are talking to, boy?" he growls into my ear while swinging at me furiously.

He gets a couple good jabs in, but I barely feel those. I grab his fists and twist his arms until he grunts in pain, then I kick his legs out from under him. He falls to the floor with a hard thud, and a thunderous feeling encompasses me.

Grabbing a fistful of his hair with my left hand, I hold his head in place and pull my other hand back. I make a tight fist and slam into his jaw, hitting him over and over again.

Eventually, he stops struggling, and after a few punches, his body goes limp in my hold.

I snarl, angry he's such a piece of shit, he couldn't even stay awake. My muscles are burning from excursion, air fills my lungs, but I don't fully breathe. Every time I think of pulling away, I see Elyse and her beautiful face covered in blood and continue punching him until his face is completely unrecognizable. "How dare you fucking touch her!" I seethe into the nothingness. "You piece of shit!" I yell. I push onto my feet and start kicking him, wishing he'd wake the hell up so I could do it all over again.

Blood drips off my hands onto the floor—and I enjoy it. I enjoyed killing him, more than I enjoyed killing my stepfather. I smile, staring down at his pathetic body. I don't even hear Damon come in, so when he appears from around the corner, I lunge at him. It takes me a moment to get my bearings as Damon's words echo through my mind.

"Jesus fuck, Hero! We've got him. Go get Elyse." He shoves in the opposite direction of my father's body.

It occurs to me I never asked him where she was.

I run out of the room and start searching through the entire house. "Elyse!" I call out her name, over and over again.

Dread creeps in, and I worry he may have killed her. I keep running from room to room, yelling her name. Then a door under the staircase catches my eye. Of course, the fucking basement.

I rip the door open so harshly, the old piece of shit comes off its hinges. I fly down the stairs and come to a sudden halt on the bottom step. I wish more than anything I could un-see what I'm seeing right now.

Her small fragile body sits in a wooden chair, her limbs tied with rope, her beautiful face swollen, bloodied, and beaten.

She doesn't move, not even as I walk toward her. Her head remains hanging to the side and those beautiful blue eyes I love so much are firmly closed.

Staring at her there, I think she might be dead, and in that second, I know I won't walk out of this house alive if it's true. If she is dead, my life is over.

A low whimper is what makes me take another step forward. I kneel in front of her, afraid to touch her, afraid I may hurt her even more. "Elyse? Please, baby, can you hear me?"

She tries to open her eyes, but she's too weak. "Hero?"

Her angel voice is low and raspy, but it's the most beautiful sound I've heard in my entire life. I move behind her and retrieve my pocket knife, then start cutting through the rope. "I'm here, baby. I'm so sorry. I am so fucking sorry. I'm going to get you out of here, okay? Hang on. We'll get you to a hospital. I'll make this right. I'll never let you go again—never."

The moment I free her from the restraints, she falls forward, her body too weak to even sit up on her own. I catch her and pull her into my chest. Overcome with emotions I don't understand, I begin to sob.

I hear footsteps behind me and shift to face whoever it is.

I'll kill them. All of them.

"She's okay, man. She's okay." Damon's voice fills the room.

My saddened gaze slips down over Elyse, taking in her broken features. "She's not okay..." My voice cracks as more tears slide down my cheeks. "She's not okay." I dismiss Damon and start up the stairs. My eyes remain on Elyse, my ears listening to the dull thump of her heart.

"No one will ever hurt you again. No one," I whisper, kissing her softly on her cheek.

24

lyse

THERE'S A BLINDING light that tries to enter my eyes every time they flutter. Oh, how I wish the morning sunlight would just go away. I shift against the bed sheets. My body aches so badly. I halt my movements and try to open my eyes. It takes an immense amount of energy to get them open, but when I do, everything comes rushing back to me.

The basement. Hero's father. The horrible things he did to me. My parents. A machine beside me beeps, getting louder and louder. I move my gaze toward it and realize I'm in a hospital.

Machines surround me, and needles poke into my arm. My wrist is no longer in a brace. It is in an actual cast now. I scan the room for someone and find Hero sitting on a chair beside me.

His eyes are closed, and his head is resting on his own shoulder. As if he senses me looking at him in his sleep, his eyes pop open and his dark gaze locks on mine. There're bluish bags underneath his eyes, telling me he's had a sleepless night or two. He sits up in his chair and reaches for my hand. My fingers inch toward him, but that little bit of movement is enough to cause me pain.

I wince, grinding my teeth together to hold back the anguish wanting to escape my lips.

"Baby, don't move, okay?"

Hero's voice sounds almost foreign. I've never heard him sound so concerned and pained before. "I'm sorry, Elyse—so fucking sorry for all of this. If I'd just stayed. If I'd just told you no, and pushed back, you wouldn't be here right now."

I shake my head at him and try to talk. My mouth opens, but I can't push out the words. Looking around, I search for something to drink.

Hero gets up and grabs a cup of water sitting on the little slide out table for me.

Holding it to my lips, I suck greedily from the straw. Cool water touches my cracked, dry lips, and I guzzle down the drink like it's the best thing I've ever had.

When my throat finally feels somewhat normal, I try to talk again. "Hero—this is not your fault." The words finally come out, but I have to take a little break in between. Even talking is hard labor. "Please—don't blame yourself."

My mind slowly drifts to the people responsible for my kidnapping.

My own parents.

I hate them. I never thought the day would come when I would feel that way, but it has.

"If I would have listened to you and stayed home, this wouldn't have happened. There are so many what ifs. You can't claim full responsibility when it wasn't all your fault."

He shakes his head like he doesn't want to listen to anything I have to say.

Like always, I know how stubborn and set in his ways he can be. But I'm stubborn too, and there's no way I'm letting him take the blame on this.

He lets out a heavy sigh. "Still, if I wouldn't have entered your life, you wouldn't be in this hospital bed right now. If I stay out of your life from here on out, you'll have a better future. I know it, and I'm sure you know it too, you just don't want to admit it."

His words shock me so much, I try to sit up. A sharp, radiating pain fills my body, reminding me of my injuries. "What are you saying, Hero?" I'm afraid to even ask.

"I'm saying I'm going to do the right thing and leave as soon as you're better and out of here."

His words hurt more than the current pain I'm feeling.

"Don't worry, though. I can give you some money, so you don't have to work while you're in school. I always told you I'd take care of you, and I'll help you out financially, but that has to be it. I can't do the love, the touching and kissing. I can't have you, Elyse. After this, I'll stay out of your life."

"I don't want your money," I growl, angry he even brought money into this conversation. I could be dirt poor and on the street, and I'd still choose him over anything else. "I want you."

"I'm not good enough for you." He holds his head in his hands, his fingers threading through his dark locks.

"Stop it!"

Hero's head snaps up at my loud voice. I'm proud of myself, of how strong I sound. "Stop telling yourself you are not good enough. There is no one better for me than you! Don't you get that? We belong together."

Hero looks at me, and I can see the exact moment he starts believing it too, believes he is good enough for me.

He's always thought the worst of himself, but I refuse to let him think that way anymore. He's everything I want and need.

"I love you, Elyse, so fucking much. I love you so damn

much, it hurts me. It fucking hurts me to think of losing you again. I cannot lose you again. I can't." He leans in to kiss me.

His lips are so gentle and soft, I want to deepen the kiss. A dark stubble covers Hero's face. It's the very first time I've noticed it since I woke up. "I love you too," I tell him, nuzzling into his cheek. His touch makes me feel alive.

Our little moment is interrupted with a soft knock against the door. When neither of us say anything, the door opens, and a woman pops her head into the room. She smiles when she sees me looking at her. "You're awake." She is way too damn happy for someone like me. She opens the door the rest of the way, putting the door stop into place before walking inside.

I take in her light green scrubs and the stethoscope hanging around her neck. My eyes catch on her nametag. Dr. White. I watch her as she casually grabs a clipboard hanging from the bottom of my bed.

Her eyes go to whatever is written on the clipboard, then she starts talking, "Elyse, my name is Dr. White. I've been overseeing your care for the last five days."

Five days! What the hell have I been doing for five days?

"It looks like you have been healing well. Are you in any pain right now?"

I blink, completely forgetting her previous question. "Wait, did you just say five days?" My gaze swings to Hero, and he shrugs, like he doesn't have a clue why I'm upset. Five days is a long time to just be sleeping in a hospital bed, doing nothing.

"Yes." She smiles at me like this is completely normal. "Don't worry. You went through a very traumatic experience. Your body needed the rest, so we made the decision to put you into a medically induced coma to help you heal faster. You are doing well now and should be able to go home in a few days."

I feel a little less tense hearing her say that, but going home...scares me.

"Now that you are up, we are going to run a few more tests

and make sure everything is all right. We've also got you going home on some prescriptions."

"Okay," is all I can say. What else am I supposed to say? This entire thing is a mess. I just want to go home and crawl in bed with Hero.

What happened to Hero's dad? My parents? How did Hero find me? After she leaves, I turn my attention back to Hero. "Hero, what happened to your father?" Just thinking about him makes my stomach churn, the contents threatening to come up. Watching Hero's face fall at the mention of his dad lets me know he feels the same way.

"Don't worry about it, baby. You never have to worry about him again. He'll never hurt you or anyone else. He is gone."

"Gone? Like in jail?" The thought of him going to jail doesn't really sit well with me. It sounds more like a free ride for him than anything.

"No, Elyse. He's dead," he says the words without showing any emotion. "I killed him."

To my utter surprise, my first thought is Hero might go back to prison. I'm not scared or shocked. Above all, I'm scared to lose Hero. "What about the police? Does anyone know?" I whisper, like someone might be listening from the corner of the room.

"Damon took care of it," is all he offers.

I decide to leave it at that. I really don't want to know any of the details. I'm just glad he is gone and Hero is safe. Maybe all can finally be right in the world again.

"Your parents stopped by to see you."

My eyes go wide at his words.

"I didn't let them in, though. I didn't think you'd want them here, so I sent them away. I also may have threatened them." He gives me a pant-melting smile that leaves me weak in the knees.

"Good, I never want to see them again. I never want to be in the same room with them again. I hate them. I truly do!" The image of my mother walking away from me, leaving me in that basement will haunt me forever.

"Did you know they were there? They came to get me. I begged them, Hero. I begged for her to stay, and she left—walked right up the stairs. She fucking left me there." Emotions swirl out of control inside me. It's like a raging wildfire is taking place and I have nowhere to escape from getting burnt.

Hero nods, and his jaw tightens. His emerald green eyes fill with a fury that matches my own. "Well, you don't have to see them ever again. If that's what you want, baby, I'll make sure of it."

I hold Hero's hand in mine and thank god I'm here with him. That I can feel his touch, that he made it to me in time.

We sit in a comfortable silence for a long while.

The nurse comes in a short time later and takes me off some of the machines so I can start getting up and moving around. I'm still sore all over, but being able to walk around the halls and to the cafeteria is nice.

Even nicer is when Hero helps me into the shower. He washes me from top to bottom, taking care of me better than any nurse ever could. By the time I'm done, I feel ten times better. I catch a glimpse of myself in the mirror. Most of my injuries are purple and green partially healed bruises.

Hero presses kisses against the entire side of my face, telling me how perfect I am.

As promised, the doctor runs more tests on me, taking blood samples, urine samples. Like I haven't been poked with needles and ordered around enough already.

By the end of the day, I'm so tired of this hospital, I just want to go back to Hero's place. I want to go home. After nagging the doctor and nurses all day, I'm told I can go home in the morning if all my bloodwork comes back normal.

When I'm too exhausted to keep my eyes open any longer, Hero folds open the recliner next to my bed and lies down on it.

"I can't wait to sleep in bed next to you," I mumble, my eyes heavy. Hero's hand remains in mine, centering me, reminding me I'm not alone and never will be.

"Tomorrow, baby. Tomorrow," he whispers, moving enough to press his lips against my forehead. "I love you, Elyse. I love you so much."

His *I love yous* are like a lullaby lulling me into a restful sleep.

~

I'M WOKEN in the morning by a soft knock I'm already familiar with. It's Dr. White. As soon as I realize it's her, I'm wide awake sitting straight up in bed, a smile lining my lips. "Please tell me you are here to let me know all my bloodwork is good and I can go home?"

Hero stirs beside me, probably from the excitement zinging through me.

"I did get your bloodwork back and you are very healthy and ready to go home."

I sigh in relief at her words.

"But before I can release you, I need to talk to you about something I noticed when I was looking at your results."

"What's wrong?" Hero asks the question running through my head. He's now sitting straight up, his eyes open wide, as he waits for her next words.

"Well, nothing is wrong...not really. It's just that you are pregnant. Very early stages, but we were able to detect the hormone change in your blood already."

I keep blinking as if to make sure I'm not imagining this. It takes a minute for what she just said to sink in. "Pregnant? Like a baby?" My words are shaky.

"Yes." She chuckles. "Pregnant, as in *you* are having a baby. I know you're young and you might be overwhelmed by all of this right now, but trust me, you are going to be fine."

"Of course she'll be fine." Hero takes my small hand in both of his larger ones and makes me turn to him. "Elyse, you'll be more than fine. You'll be the best mother the world has ever seen, and I'll try my fucking hardest to be the best father I can be. I'll always take care of you and our baby. Always."

Tears start to fall from my eyes. I can't even come up with the words I want to describe this moment. My heart is so full of love, it might explode.

I smile. Of course Hero will take care of me and our baby.

I love him, and he loves me. After all we've been through, whatever happens from here on out, he'll always be...

My hero.

EPILOGUE

3 Months Later
Hero

I CRADLED her small bump in my hands. I'd never considered becoming a father with my upbringing, but I had pushed all that aside, knowing I had to be whatever I could for Elyse and our unborn baby.

Since the moment we left the hospital, Elyse was in my care. She went to her classes, and Tasha eventually warmed up to me. I apologized to her for my behavior, and after seeing me take care of Elyse, she started to come around more often. In the end, she had the best interests for Elyse, but that didn't mean I liked her snubbing her nose at me.

Elyse's parents tried to contact her one more time after we got home from the hospital. I answered her phone and told them she was pregnant. He mom hung up and we haven't heard from them since. Hopefully, we won't hear from them ever again.

I had refused to let Elyse go back to doing tutoring sessions.

Her safety was my biggest priority, and I couldn't have her sitting with some random guy in a room by herself for an hour, even more so now that she was pregnant.

I didn't think it was possible, but ever since I found out she was carrying our child, my obsession to keep her safe, keep *them* safe, has grown out of control. I'm even more possessive, terrified of someone hurting her, taking her. She doesn't seem to mind, though—which is good. I cannot rein in those feelings, not after all she's endured.

"Do you have any names you like?" Her voice sounds as sweet as honey.

I love hearing her talk. She could be reading the grocery list and I wouldn't give a fuck. I just want to hear her talk. "If it's a girl, I would like to name her Isabelle. That was my mother's name."

"Isabelle," she repeats, like she's trying it out. "I like it. What if it's a boy?"

"How about Dragon Slayer?" I grin at her.

Elyse's giggle fills the bedroom. "How about Isabelle if it's a girl, and if it's a boy, I pick a name. I hate to say it, but it's not going to be anything even remotely close to Dragon Slayer."

I nod. "That sounds good to me. Now, how about I go get you some ice cream?"

"I'm not in the mood for ice cream."

"No? Pickles then? Wait, pickles and peanut butter again?" I've always thought people made up the myth of pregnant women having these crazy cravings. Turns out, they didn't. Elyse has eaten some of the weirdest shit I have ever heard of.

"Nope, I'm in the mood for something else. You." Her small body moves on top of mine, straddling me.

Fuck. My cock responds immediately, as if it's in tune with every single word she says.

Until Elyse got pregnant, I wasn't even aware of increased

libido being a pregnancy symptom. But now, I'm very familiar with that symptom and all too happy to bend to her needs.

The grind of her sweet pussy against my rock-hard dick pulls me from my thoughts. Her pussy is always dripping with need, ready whenever I want her. If there weren't any clothes between us, I would have already slipped deep inside her tight hole. I let her move like that for a short time, watching her through hooded eyes, her perky breasts spilling out of the top of her bra. She is beautiful, and I crave her body like it's my next fucking hit.

Having had enough of this torture, I roll us over so she's on her back.

She looks up at me with adoration and love.

God, my chest fucking tightens, my stomach knotting. I'll never get over the way she looks at me. Like I'm her entire world or something...

Cupping her cheek, I lean into her, making sure I don't squish her growing stomach. I make quick work of her sleep shorts and toss them over my shoulder behind me.

Her legs spread apart, giving me access to her glistening wet center. I groan, my eyes roaming over the sweet honey that drips from her tight entrance. I lift my gaze back up to her and see her nibbling on her bottom lip.

She looks like a little fucking siren—tempting and teasing me in the way only she can. "I love you," she nearly whispers.

I pull away for a second to free myself of my shorts. "I love you too, baby. More than anything." Using one arm, I hold my weight and fist my throbbing cock in my hand. My chest fills with air as I press my hips close to her center, my thickness sliding smoothly into her warm depths.

She moans out in pleasure, her cerulean blue eyes full of desire.

I still inside her for a moment, relishing in the way she tightens around me, the way her pussy claims me like it's meant for me and only me. "You feel like heaven," I hiss out, pulling out an inch before I thrust back in. My forehead rests against hers, and our pants of pleasure mingle together as I fuck her slowly. I claim her over and over again with each thrust.

She meets me thrust for thrust, her hips pushing up. "Hero," my name falls from her lips like a plea.

I up my pace just a little more, my cock bottoming out inside her. With one hand on her hip to hold her in place, I swivel my hips just as I reach the back of her channel. The pierced tip of my cock hits her sweet spot every time. After a few more thrusts, her tiny nails are sink into my flesh as her breaths become ragged. Her pussy pulsates around me, strangling the ever-loving life out of me.

"Oh god...oh god..." she cries out.

I smile, pressing a hard kiss to her lips before I up my pace once more. I'm fucking her hard, but not hard enough.

Her eyes flutter open and stare into mine.

I'm barely holding myself together, the need to drive into her nearly overtaking me. "I need to fuck you harder, but I don't want to hurt the baby..." This is something I've dealt with over the last three months. Feelings overtake me without warning and make me feel like a little boy unsure of what to do.

"You know you won't. I trust you, Hero. I love you," Elyse rasps, her hand cupping my cheek.

She's looking at me like I make the sun rise and fall, and I know I won't let her down. Gritting my teeth, I stare into her eyes, my eyes watching for any pain in her features as I increase my pace.

When I see nothing but desire, love, and understanding, I enter her harder. I will never understand how she can have so much trust in me. She trusts and believes in me when no one else does, when no one else ever did—not even myself.

I drive into her as deep and fast as I can. Watching her come apart beneath me again sends me headfirst into my own release.

It starts with a tingle in my spine that spreads throughout my entire body in seconds. It sets every single fiber in my body on fire and makes every muscle lock up before allowing the tension to release. My chest heaves, and my grip on Elyse tightens. I never want to leave the confines of her pussy.

I'm sent to heaven and back, my body slowly floating back down to earth and into the arms of an angel—my angel.

"You're my hero, and you'll be our baby's hero someday too."

Elyse's voice touches something inside me. Her words snap me in two, the contents of my heart spilling out, pulsing like a wound that won't stop bleeding. I take her tiny hand and press it against my erratic heartbeat. Her fingers splay against my skin, the warmth of my body seeping right into hers.

I stare deeply into her eyes as I say the next set of words. "I vow to always protect you, cherish you, and be the man you need me to be. I'll always love and support you, and I'll do whatever I can to make you and our baby happy. We might have met by accident, but I'm convicted to a lifetime sentence."

Tears fall from Elyse's eyes, her head nodding in understanding. "I know—I've known all along."

And all over again, she reminds me of the belief she's always had in me.

Thank you for reading the Convict Me! If you can't get enough of these character, don't worry they make plenty of appearances in our other books. Follow the Rossi Crime Family and in Damon's book **Protect Me**.
(A Dark Mafia Romance)

Keep reading for previews...

PREVIEW OF PROTECT ME

Chapter One
Keira

I stare at my brother's lifeless body on the floor of my apartment. I know what I need to do next, but I can't move. My feet remain cemented to the floor as my eyes move over the scene before me. There's so much blood.

I bite my bottom lip hard enough to draw my own blood. I won't scream. I can't. Leo had told me if someone ever came for him, I was to go to someone and they would protect me, but I can't remember their name.

My stomach rolls, bile rising into my throat. I place a hand over my mouth to stop the impending vomit.

My brother is dead. My chest tightens, and I fist my hands at my sides. My brother is dead. Actually dead. We had joked about this moment so many, but looking down at his lifeless body, his vacant stare...this isn't a joke.

Start moving, a little voice inside my head reminds me.

I look at the message the bastards left on my fridge. The sticky note shakes in my hands as I read the words.

I'll be back for you.

I shiver involuntarily. I need to find the guy my brother wanted me to go to. He may be the only one who can protect me now.

With unsteady hands, I pull my phone out and go to my emergency information. I had created a small doc. Leo only gave me a name and address, stating it would be enough.

But how can I just show up on someone's doorstep with this kind of thing? Leo told me the person would understand, they'd know why I was there, but I don't believe that. Too afraid to go into my bedroom or even stand inside the kitchen another minute, I walk out the door, closing it quietly behind me.

Tears fall from my eyes, staining my cheeks. I've never felt so much pain and confusion all at once. My lungs seem to deflate, refusing to fill no matter how many breaths I take.

I make it two steps down the stairs when I hear voices from the level below me. I spot two guys talking. They have accents. Russian maybe? I'm not all that concerned with them until their words meet my ears. Frozen in place, I listen more intently.

"The boss said he wants the sister for himself, so don't fuck her up too bad." The men are big and burly, way bigger than me, and definitely stronger. If they get their hands on me, I'm as good as gone.

Move, Kiera! With my brother's voice filling my head, I tried to relax my tense muscles. I have to get out of here. If they catch me... I shove the thought away before it takes root.

As soft as my feet let me, I tiptoe away from the staircase. Slipping my shoes off, I walk up the stairs in my socks, staying close to the outside, making sure they can't see me.

With my lip caught between my teeth, I hold in the scream wanting to rip from my throat. Fear consumes me. My muscles remain rigid, but I continue onward. I walk all the way to the top floor and took the emergency stairwell down.

I'll be safe, hidden from their gazes, a secret just passing through. My entire body shakes as I take two steps at a time, my eyes passing over my shoulder every few seconds, thus causing me to trip. I land against the railing, and it digs painfully into my ribs. I need to pay better attention, otherwise, I'm going to get myself caught.

I sigh in relief when I make it down the stairs fully. I'm only in my first year of college. I'm supposed to be partying, hanging out with other people my age, not discovering my dead brother's body or running away from monsters who want to drag me back to their boss. The image of being attacked by one of them flickers in my mind.

No. I will myself to calm down. I'm hanging on the very edge of losing control. I want to cry, scream, yell, but I know none of those things will happen. Pushing through the back doors of the apartment complex, I run down the street, my backpack still resting heavily against my back.

I sprint down the street a ways and hide behind a group of trees before I decide to catch my breath. My little legs do nothing to help me when it comes to running. I pull out my cell phone and enter the address into the map.

A little icon pops up on the screen confirming it was working. I sag against the tree, waiting for it to load.

Could they track my phone? How did they know my brother? Who were they? A dozen questions rattle off inside my head. I hadn't even said goodbye to him. My gaze dropped down to my phone and I notice the map had finally loaded.

Fear pumps through my veins, hopefully, whoever I was going to see who know more than I did about the situation. Otherwise, I was kind of screwed.

The idea of being caught by those sinister men, made me move faster. My map pinpointed the location at something called Night Shift. Whatever the hell that was. I don't really care where the place is, all I want to do is get there.

After walking for what seemed like forever, I arrive at the building, my eyes glossing over it. I clench my jaw in anger.

This is a strip club... I know so because there was a sign hanging plastered to the front window on the door that said NOW HIRING: BEST STRIPPERS IN THE AREA.

My mouth goes dry. Why did my brother send me to a strip club? Was this some kind of sick joke, a chance for him to get back at me after death? I wouldn't work here, not ever. Shivering I grew afraid of the idea of going inside there. Who did I ask for? What if they told me to leave? I wrap my arms around myself, a cold breeze blowing through me.

Go inside. The same voice from earlier demands. I know I'm slightly unhinged, even more so if I'm hearing things inside my head, but I know it was my bodies warning, my bodies way of making me do something I didn't want to because I was too scared.

Dragging my feet across the concrete I grip the metal door, the cold of it radiating through my body, making all the warmth inside me dissipate.

I open the first door, and then a second door, my feet moving all on their own. I'm shaking like a damn leaf in the wind. I want to rewind time and go back to this morning when my brother was alive and joking with me.

When my feet stop moving, I realize I was at the bar. The inside wasn't as bad as I thought it'd be. A huge stage with a large seating area was on the other side of the room. There's a long hallway off to the left, and then the bar which I was standing at.

"If you're looking for the boss, he's in his office." I licked my lips nervously, swallowing some of the fear down.

"Which way?" I barely got the words out. The woman in front of me eyes me curiously, her hazel eyes piercing mine. She looks to be ten years older than me, her face is dolled up with makeup and she's wearing hardly any clothing. Her breasts are all but falling out of her top, and the shirt if you could even call it one covers only half of her stomach.

If she wore a bathing suit it would have covered more skin.

"Down the hall that way," She hooks a thumb in the direction of the hallway off to the left. "Then follow it until the very end and turn left. You'll see a big man standing outside his office, that's how you'll know you made it." The mystery woman smiles warmly.

I nod and head off in the direction she said. My legs quivered, and fear of the unknown slithers up my spine. I don't know what I was walking into. From the looks of the place, women were nothing more than an object, and I didn't want to be an object, not for anyone. I didn't even want to be looked at, let alone touched.

Again, I questioned why my brother had sent me here?

Walking down the dimly lit hall I follow the woman's orders, passing numerous wooden doors. A couple of moans and screams have me scurrying faster, my feet slipping all over the floor. When I make it to the end of the hall I turn left and stop as there was nowhere else to go. There is a door directly in front of me, but there is no man standing outside of it.

Am I in the right spot?

I walk up to the door, my hand reaching out to trace the letter engraved into it.

DAMON ROSSI.

I blink slowly below his name was one single word:

BOSS.

My stomach churns and I press my hand against the door more firmly to hold myself up. I was going to pass out. I knew it. Today had pushed me beyond my limits. I was scared out of my mind and had nowhere else to go. I guess I could go back home and be killed or worse off caught by those bastards. Or I could get my shit together and walk inside that office and find out who Damon Rossi was to my brother. Taking a calming breath,

I grab hold of the brass knob and turn it slowly. I hold my breath as I push the door open a low creaking sound emitting from the damn thing. I exhale a moment later and poke my head inside. Scanning the room and listening for any sounds I step inside the office.

I can't help but feel like a rabbit caught in a snare. Like something bad is about to happen?

My heart is racing, and my palms are sweaty. I feel like an intruder, but I force myself to stay put. My brother wouldn't have sent me here if he didn't think I'd be safe, right? The fact that I need to find out who Damon is, pushes me onward. I let my backpack slide off my shoulder and deposit it onto the chair in front of the desk.

My fingers trail against the mahogany wood, and I walk around the room taking it in, in its entirety. There're pictures on the walls, paperwork everywhere. There is a manliness about the room, and I don't know how to describe it.

It's dark, and sinister, and smells like tobacco and whiskey. I look at the files that lay on his desk. There are girls' names written on the front of each folder and I open one of them up out of pure curiosity. I gasp, and close it shut as soon as I see the picture of a naked woman posing in a very provocative position.

My gaze drops to a drawer under the desk. I know I shouldn't be snooping, and I don't really know what I'm looking for, but I feel the need to search...for something...anything. I reach for the handle, but when I try to pull it open, I realize it's locked.

Looking around the room, disappointed, I realize there is nothing else for me to find in here. Walking back around the desk, I'm about to sit down on the couch pushed up against the wall when I feel the air shift in the room.

There's a warmth that fills the air...a warmth that carries a dark feel.

My heart beats a million miles per minute, and the hair on

the back my neck stands up. I feel like I've escaped one monster only to be trapped by another.

I'm frozen, too terrified to move when I hear someone behind me. I suck in a sharp breath, building the shrill scream in my throat. I feel hands on me. The roughness of his touch is unforgiving.

Before my scream can make its appearance, I'm pushed down face first onto the couch, struggling to breathe. I try to get up, but he leans his much larger body into mine, making it impossible for me to move. His grip is relentless, and when I feel something hard pressing against my ass, I gasp.

No. No. No.

"I don't usually fuck women in here, but since you seem so interested in my office, I suppose I should give you the grand tour while you ride my cock."

My eyes squeeze shut, my body freezes, and I become so tense, my body starts to ache. My brother sent me to be raped? Tears prick my eyes. My yoga pants are ripped down my legs, and I start to shake, my body sinking deeper into the cushion. I want the moment to be over. I bite the inside of my cheek. The copper taste of blood fills my mouth.

"If you want the job, you can't be so tense. No one wants to fuck a piece of board," a dark voice whispers into my hair. A shudder runs through my entire body. I'm not sure I'll ever get his voice out of my head again...

Find Protect Me on Amazon

ABOUT THE AUTHORS

J.L. Beck and C. Hallman are an international bestselling author duo who write contemporary and dark romance.

For a list of all of our books, updates and freebies visit our website.

www.bleedingheartromance.com

ALSO BY THE AUTHORS

CONTEMPORAY ROMANCE

North Woods University
The Bet
The Dare
The Secret
The Vow
The Promise
The Jock

Bayshore Rivals
When Rivals Fall
When Rivals Lose
When Rivals Love

Breaking the Rules
Kissing & Telling
Babies & Promises
Roommates & Thieves

Also by the Authors

DARK ROMANCE

The Blackthorn Elite
Hating You
Breaking You
Hurting You
Regretting You

The Obsession Duet
Cruel Obsession
Deadly Obsession

The Rossi Crime Family
Protect Me
Keep Me
Guard Me
Tame Me
Remember Me

The Moretti Crime Family
Savage Beginnings
Violent Beginnings

The King Crime Family
Indebted
Inevitable

STANDALONES

Their Captive

Runaway Bride

His Gift

Also by the Authors

Convict Me

Two Strangers

Manufactured by Amazon.ca
Bolton, ON